ECHO *on the* BAY

ECHO *on the* BAY

MASATSUGU ONO

Translated from Japanese by ANGUS TURVILL

TWO LINES
PRESS

Originally published as: にぎやかな湾に背負われた船
(*Nigiyakana wan ni seowareta fune*)
Copyright © 2015 by Masatsugu Ono
Original Japanese edition published by Asahi Shimbun
Publications Inc.
This English edition is published by arrangement with Asahi
Shimbun Publications Inc., Tokyo
in care of Tuttle-Mori Agency, Inc., Tokyo.
Translation © 2020 by Angus Turvill

Two Lines Press
582 Market Street, Suite 700, San Francisco, CA 94104
www.twolinespress.com

ISBN 978-1-949641-03-5
Ebook ISBN 978-1-949641-04-2

Library of Congress Cataloging-in-Publication Data:
Names: Ono, Masatsugu, 1970– author. | Turvill, Angus, translator.
Title: Echo on the bay / Masatsugu Ono; translated by Angus Turvill.
Other titles: Nigiyakana wan ni seowareta fune. English
Description: San Francisco: Two Lines Press, [2020]
Summary: "Tells the story of a small fishing village in Japan--with the
untreated wounds of the town's history in the foreground"-- Provided
by publisher. | Identifiers: LCCN 2019044396
ISBN 9781949641035 (paperback) | ISBN 9781949641042 (ebook)
Classification: LCC PL874.N64 N5413 2020 | DDC 895.63/6--dc23
LC record available at https://lccn.loc.gov/2019044396

Cover design by Gabriele Wilson
Cover photo © Elsa Leydier / Millennium Images, UK
Design by Sloane | Samuel
Printed in the United States of America

1 3 5 7 9 10 8 6 4 2

This project is supported in part by an award from
the National Endowment for the Arts.

ART WORKS.
arts.gov

Dad had a lot of things bothering him when he was stationed on the coast.

There was the abandoned boat floating in the bay. There was the body that Mitsugu Azamui said was on the beach, but which nobody had ever found. There were the boys who kept shooting bottle rockets at old Toshiko-bā's house. And then there was me, in love with Mr. Yoshida, my social studies teacher.

"Looks like we'll be able to get a new car!" Dad said, seeing how fed up Mom looked when he told her about the move.

Mom was worried about my private high school entrance exams. In the city, I'd been going to a well-known cram school in the evenings and was due to join the advanced group when I got to second year. Down on the coast there was no such thing as a cram school.

Dad wasn't exactly against me going to a private high school, but he took no interest in the idea.

"A public school will be fine," he said. "They're all

the same in the end. Look at me. I never went near a private school, but I'm looking after you all well enough!"

Dad often said that kind of thing, ignoring the fact that he'd always failed his promotion exams and was set to spend his whole career on the bottom rung. His self-confidence unsettled Mom and made her set all the more importance on my exams.

Dad had been in a good mood ever since he'd been told about the transfer. His head was full of this new car idea. In fact, upgrading was standard behavior among his colleagues. Whenever any of them was re-posted a long way off they always used their relocation allowances to buy a better car. Mr. Yamamoto, whom Dad was replacing, had come back to the city with a Nissan Cima.

"Yamamoto's got GPS!" Dad exclaimed. "What's the use of GPS in a place like that? There's only one road. Not a single traffic light."

"The work's easy," Mr. Yamamoto told Dad. "Nothing to worry about."

It was the day before we were set to leave and there was stuff all over the floor.

"Nothing serious happens," he said. "You won't get any burglaries. You may have to grab up a high school kid now and then for stealing dried squid, but that's about it. Nobody even bothers to lock up at night or when they go out. I sometimes went inside people's houses to turn off their lights when there was nobody there. I suppose I could have been arrested for unlawful entry! But the people there don't get worked up

4

about a thing like that," he laughed, pulling a piece of packing tape off his sock. "The only problem is it's so small. You see the same people all the time and you get too close to them. You'll have somebody drinking at your house every single night."

It was just as Mr. Yamamoto said. Almost every day when I got home from volleyball, I'd find Mitsugu Azamui in the living room, drinking. He'd be sitting cross-legged on the floor opposite Dad. His thin body was always bent so far forward that it looked like he was drinking directly from the tabletop. From time to time he'd look up at Dad, as if suddenly remembering that someone was with him. His eyes were cloudy and yellow. My eight-year-old brother, Keiji, was scared of him and wouldn't come into the living room. He'd peer in from the kitchen looking miserable. "I wanna watch TV!" he'd snivel to Mom.

Mitsugu Azamui was one of the village celebrities. He drank all day every day and had sold his house to pay for it. His wife and children had left him long ago. Now he was living in public housing on the far side of the creek that ran past the police house. The reason he didn't have to work was that he got disability payments for hand-arm vibration syndrome. He'd been a construction worker when he was younger, moving from one tunnel site to the next.

He'd come over to our house, drink, and talk about a body that had washed up on the beach. Nobody but him had ever seen it.

"Ain't no use believin' a drunk like him," the villagers warned Dad.

His hands were always shaking. You couldn't be sure whether it was vibration syndrome or alcohol that did it. Each of his fingers shook like the needle of a broken compass, one that sent the traveler around in a circle and back to his starting point. People who'd gone to see the traveler off grew weary of his constant returns. And this particular traveler was no hero. He'd endured no real defeats, exhausted by an endless struggle against barriers (the enemy without) and hesitation (the enemy within). No, he was just a tottering drunk with a limitless thirst for alcohol. The local people had grown tired of Mitsugu Azamui long ago because of the way he came to their houses and drank their liquor without paying a penny for it. That's why he was now drinking at an outsider's house, Dad's house.

He never looked happy when he was drinking. I watched him from the far end of the room. The drunker he got, the more rigid and expressionless his face became. It lost its connection with time—an ageless profile, like a face stamped on a coin, unearthed among the remnants of a minor kingdom that no longer existed. The king had been deposed and the country gone to ruin, but the faces on the coins knew nothing of that. Gradually, the features of the faces faded, their outlines were lost, and they disappeared one by one into a smooth oblivion.

Mitsugu Azamui seemed an odd name. I asked Mr. Yoshida if he knew why people called him that. Mr. Yoshida, besides being the social studies teacher, also taught physical education and was our volleyball coach. He was twenty-four and had been brought up in the village. He told me they'd always used the name when he was a boy, just as they did now.

Apparently, it had originated a long time ago. After the war, soldiers from the occupation forces came to the village. Somebody told the children that Americans had tails, so the children chased after them, trying to see. "Typical!" laughed the local men. "Only women and children could be interested in them hairy bastards!" But their smiles disappeared when they realized just how interested the women really were. The incidence of domestic quarrels suddenly shot up.

One day, the children sneaked up to the inn where the soldiers were staying and tried to peak into the bathroom. Of course, the soldiers didn't like that and one of them got out of the water, walked straight over to the door, and flung it open. The children scattered as fast as they could, but one little boy didn't get away. He was so surprised he just fell on his butt. As he sat there almost in tears, with "America-san" looking down at him, he remembered some English phrases that he'd been taught:

"Sank you, sank you. My name is Mitsugu Azamui."

The American burst out laughing. The little boy watched as the waves of laughter made America-san's tail jolt and swing above his head.

"It were a tail, a tail!" he shouted when his friends came back. "A real long tail! And it had balls!"

After that the boy, whose name was really Azamui Mitsugu, was always called Mitsugu Azamui, in the English order, as though his given name were his surname.

About a year after we moved to the village, there was an election for the district assembly. Normally, the only sounds we heard were those of the wind over the bay and vehicles on the prefectural road that had been carved into the mountain to the west. But even here things got noisy during a campaign. Wherever you went, it was like listening to an overused cassette tape being played backward at maximum volume.

There were three candidates from the village, and to make matters worse, two of them were brothers-in-law. The resulting mayhem led to Dad getting a huge dent in his new car. Mom was mad at him about that, and Dad was miserable.

The battle between the brothers-in-law was the main focus of the campaign. Nobody paid much attention to the third candidate, which was hardly surprising since he ran in every election and always lost. He was like a drop of ink that falls from a calligraphy brush when you're writing large characters—a little spot on the paper that nobody even notices.

The candidate, Kawano Itaru, didn't seem to care what people thought of him. It was hard to tell if he wanted to be elected at all. He had no election vehicle to go around in, and no microphone either.

"It's grassroots," was how he described his campaign.

Kawano Itaru was a retired junior high school teacher. He'd never been a principal or held any other senior position; he'd just been an ordinary teacher throughout his career. Even in his retirement everyone always called him "Mr. Kawano," as though he were still a teacher.

There were certain things about Mr. Kawano's physical appearance that you couldn't help noticing. He had no nails on the fingers of his left hand; the joints of the third and fourth fingers didn't bend—the fingers stuck straight out, always facing the same direction, like two like-minded siblings. His left ear was missing—he never tried to conceal this, always keeping his white hair in a neat close crop that reminded me of a sports field on the morning after snow. People gestured at his ear when he kept putting himself forward as a candidate. "He can't hear the people's voice!" they laughed.

Mr. Kawano said it was his communism that had prevented him being promoted at school. Nobody knew if this was true.

In his campaign speeches he always emphasized the importance of education. Then he said that children must be told not to avoid Toshiko-bā, and to stop firing bottle rockets at her house. "That's the most important thing for the village," he said, "because children are the future." Was there a connection between that and communism? Nobody in the village knew enough about "communism" to be able to judge. But anyway, every one of his speeches ended with the issue of Toshiko-bā.

Mom once asked Dad about Mr. Kawano's political views.

"Well," he said. "Basically, not to, um, fire, you know, bottle rockets at Toshiko-bā's house."

Really, that's what everybody thought—that Mr. Kawano's platform was to stop fireworks being aimed at Toshiko-bā's house. You'd have to be pretty eccentric to vote for a candidate like that. And very few people did. The number of votes he got never came close to the number of hits that Toshiko-bā's house took over the course of the campaign. If he'd ever gotten that number, he'd have won easily.

The battling brothers-in-law were Todaka Yoshikazu, head of a major fishery and chairman of the local fishing co-operative, and Abe Hachiro, head of a construction company. Everyone called them Yoshi-nī (big brother Yoshi) and Hachi-nī (big brother Hachi). Hachi-nī was married to Yoshi-nī's sister, Hatsue.

Yoshi-nī had been on the district assembly for twelve years and was a prominent figure throughout the region. His company's dried horse-mackerel had been the most successful item in a campaign to promote regional products. It had even reached the food courts of department stores in Tokyo and Osaka. It was now the company's most profitable product, outstripping their farmed yellowtail.

The Marugi Fisheries processing plant was halfway along the promontory on the eastern side of the village. It was similar in size to the elementary school, which stood at the base of the promontory. I've been to the plant—Mr. Yoshida took me in his car. There were no houses beyond the school, so the paved road was just for the plant. It was better than the one that ran through the village—wide enough for the large refrigerated trucks that were always coming and going.

In front of the plant there's a wide open space paved with concrete. Gutted sardines and mackerel glint in the sunshine. Mr. Yoshida drives past the fish into the shade of the building. He parks the car beside a small forklift, next to a huge pile of empty wooden crates. I worry that they might topple over. When I get out of the car there's a dry smell, like manure. Flies buzz around my head, their abdomens and wings bright in the sunshine—rough, black beads of light.

On Sundays there's nobody at the plant. All I can hear is the hum of a huge refrigeration unit—a sound like numbness itself. My mind goes blank as I listen. Inside the building is an office, with a very large, black-leather sofa for visitors. That's our favorite place. As I squeeze the edge of the sofa, I open my eyes and look up at the wall. There are two photos hanging near the top. I see them upside down. They're jolting back and forth. One is of the imperial family. The other is of Yoshi-nī shaking hands with the prefectural governor. Like the governor, Yoshi-nī's thinning hair is slicked back over his scalp. He's fat and smiling, his chin drawn down against his neck. I feel slightly nauseous looking at him, so I close my eyes again. There are flies on my sweaty thighs and calves. They keep lifting off and resettling, sipping at the perspiration.

It was thanks to Yoshi-nī that Mr. Yoshida got through the teacher selection process. Mr. Yoshida's mother was Yoshi-nī's cousin.

"My university was a second-rate private place in Tokyo," Mr. Yoshida said, turning over the ignition. "I'd never have landed a teaching job right away without his help." The engine snarled—a deep, heavy growl that sent leaves and dust swirling through the air. "He had a word with a member of the prefectural assembly. He told me that as long as I got through the first written test, I'd be okay."

Mr. Yoshida's car was also thanks to Yoshi-nī. His mother had asked for a loan on her son's behalf and Yoshi-nī had agreed just like that. There's no way Mr. Yoshida, fresh out of college, could have bought a Nissan Skyline GTR otherwise. After we left the plant, he'd always drive me up to the little beach at the tip of the promontory.

Until that year, the only person from the village on the local assembly had been Yoshi-nī. But then Hachi-nī suddenly decided to run too. Hachi-nī had always supported Yoshi-nī before, but nobody seemed surprised by his change of heart. They'd been classmates through elementary and junior high schools, and had been friends, but deep down there'd always been a rivalry.

"Giant Baba and Antonio Hinoki," said Hidaka, comparing them to characters in the world of Japanese wrestling. Hidaka didn't say much, but the general consensus was that when he did, he was worth listening to. He, Iwaya, Hashimoto, and Someya were all in the police office together, drinking.

"Nah," said Someya flatly. "More like Butcher and Singh." Someya talked a lot, but people didn't often think much of what he said. This time, though, he seemed to have hit the mark.

The fat-faced Yoshi-nī was Abdullah the Butcher. Unlike the Butcher he did have a few strands of hair, though. Whenever these fell across his forehead, he'd look up, cross-eyed, and contort his mouth to blow them away.

Like Tiger Jeet Singh, Hachi-nī had a mustache, and his face was sallow and sharp. Singh often brought a saber into the ring with him, and Hachi-nī—whose hobby was collecting western weaponry—often stood in his garden gazing up at a saber held over his head.

The people of the village couldn't tell on the surface whether Yoshi-nī and Hachi-nī got along or not. But they were certainly reminiscent of the famous tag team.

But Yoshi-nī and his sister, Hatsue—Hachi-nī's wife—didn't get along at all. So, everybody saw the election as a kind of family feud.

Hatsue, who was the deputy chair of the local women's association, came by our house one evening. She stood at the back door, moaning about her brother. Mom looked a bit uncomfortable—it was no business of hers. "He stashes away loads of money for himself, and he bought a car for his cousin's son, but he won't lend us nothing at all. He knows construction's going through a rough patch, and that things're hard for us, but he's so greedy! And he's always got this grudge 'bout something that happened years ago. Can't hardly believe he's my brother!"

I could hear her angry voice from the kitchen.

Mom didn't know what to do. She just kept nodding and saying, "Oh dear!" Keiji was hanging around her, whining as he did every evening.

"It's not fair! Mitsugu Azamui will be here soon and I won't be able to watch TV. He's coming, right? He always does. It's not fair!"

His defeated, fretful voice was all but drowned out by the campaign cars as they drove around the village blaring out their messages. They kept at it all day every day, right up until 8 p.m., when they had to stop.

Votes were being bought in the village, but that

wasn't the real problem. Nearly every candidate in the district was doing that. The only one who didn't was Mr. Kawano. The villagers said it wasn't so much a question of him not buying them, but of not being *able* to buy them. They looked at him as though he were from some primitive tribe that had no concept of money. "I'm following communist ideals," was what Mr. Kawano had to say on the subject.

Though he was neither a teacher nor a doctor, the villagers always called my dad "sensei," or rather, "shenshei" in the local pronunciation. When the summer Bon festival came around, and at the end of the year too, he was showered with gifts—so many they didn't fit in the living room.

"It won't look too good, but there's nowhere else for them to go," he said, taking the gifts into the police office, which was attached to the house.

Of course, it wasn't just *things* that arrived. More frequent than the gifts were the endless visits by the people who gave them. I don't know what issues they came to discuss, but once they were inside, they did exactly the same as Mitsugu Azamui—they drank. But unlike Mitsugu, they didn't simply sit silently drinking only what they were offered. When the bottle was nearly empty, they calmly got up and went through to the police office to get another.

"Shenshei," they'd say, "that bottle of White Wave I gave you—it's next door, isn't it?" And they'd go get it and then keep on drinking.

"It's like I'm keeping their bottles for them," said Dad, clutching his stomach in drunken laughter.

Of course, it wasn't all like that. Sometimes

fishermen came around with something from their catch, or women brought potatoes and radishes from their fields. Hatsue sometimes came with dishes the women's association had made on a cooking day, and people often brought Dad a portion of the special food that had been prepared for a family wake or memorial service.

"Always nice to have a bit of free grub!" Dad said.

Mom glared.

"What a thing to say in front of the children!" she exclaimed.

Being the only policeman in the area, Dad always got a special invitation to school field days, and on such occasions, he would sit with the members of the district assembly. The assemblymen were, for the most part, the chairmen or directors of fishing or farming cooperatives, or heads of local construction companies.

They liked to be seen. When there was a meeting with just office staff present, they often excused themselves, citing business commitments. But they never missed an opportunity to parade in front of the public. There was only one hotel in the area with a wedding venue—the Hayasu. Every time there was a wedding, they'd be there, in VIP seating. At the district baseball tournament, there they'd be again, in the row that afforded the clearest view of the game. The same went for judo and kendo tournaments. Had there been a soccer tournament, they'd have expected the same treatment then. But sadly, with only one club in the district, there was no tournament. The absence of this priority-seating opportunity led to passionate exchanges in the assembly chamber about the importance of promoting soccer. When it came to funerals, they couldn't very well have special seating, so instead there was always a row of floral wreaths from the assemblymen, all the same size.

It was very awkward for a little village like ours to have multiple candidates in the election. It led to the opposing sides getting embroiled in a battle of accusations.

Someya was a Hachi-nī supporter. He came to the police office one day to tell Dad that Yoshi-nī was buying votes for 5,000 yen each. Hashimoto, a Yoshi-nī supporter, arrived almost at the same time.

"What're you doing here lookin' so fed up?" said Someya.

"Yoshi-nī asked me to come," replied Hashimoto.

"You mean you come to report Hachi-nī for breakin' the rules?"

"Yeah."

"I was sent by Hachi-nī," said Someya wearily.

Hashimoto nodded sympathetically.

"It's a pain, ain't it? I don't like makin' accusations!" he said.

"Want me to do it for you?" asked Someya.

"Would you?" said Hashimoto, suddenly cheering up. "But you're on his side…"

"It don't matter," said Someya. "But you can give me that!"

"This?" said Hashimoto holding up the large bottle of Kubota sake in his hand. "Yoshi-nī asked me to give it to shenshei."

"He's got style, Yoshi-nī, no question!" said Someya. "Why don't the two of us go in together and share it with shenshei?" he said, downing an imaginary cup.

"I wish they'd kept quiet about the vote-buying and just given me the drink," said Dad after Someya and Hashimoto had gone home. His face flushed, he tipped the Kubota bottle over his glass and shook it. Nothing came out.

"Selling your vote is against the law," I told Keiji. "Mr. Yoshida told us in our social studies class." Keiji was trying to make the most of his TV time, nervous that Mitsugu Azamui would come over soon. But the program had just reached a commercial break, so he looked up.

Dad sighed. "Mr. Yoshida, huh? Again… Well, he's right. But everyone does it around here, so there's no point in making a fuss. What good is there in trying to get each other into trouble?"

"But selling your vote is a crime," I said.

"Yeah, a crime!" said Keiji, coming over next to me. "A crime!"

"Everyone does it," said Dad, going into the kitchen. "I must have a word with Mr. Yoshida…"

"Everyone?" I said. "Mitsugu Azamui doesn't."

At the mention of Mitsugu Azamui, Keiji looked up uneasily.

"Well, he's hardly likely to go and vote, is he?" said Dad, coming back from the kitchen with two cans of beer. "But I suppose if someone offered him money, he'd take it anyway to spend on booze," he laughed as he pulled the ring on one of the cans. Beer fizzed out.

Perhaps Dad was right. I couldn't imagine Mitsugu casting a vote. The only picture that came to my mind was him drunkenly sipping *shochu*.

"If he accepted the money, I'd have to arrest him, along with everyone else in the village." Dad raised his voice and lifted his arms as though about to grab me: "Mitsugu Azamui, you are under arrest on suspicion of corruption and drunkenness!"

I froze. He veered away and brought his hands down on Keiji instead.

"Agh!" Keiji shouted and dashed into the kitchen.

"Hey!" Mom shouted. "Don't mess around like that! He'll have an asthma attack!"

The war between the two electoral camps continued. Even Yoshi-nī and Hachi-nī themselves rang Dad up to demand arrests. In the end, Dad could no longer just smile placidly and hope things would calm down. It was getting difficult to keep both sides happy, and he was constantly being accused of bias.

"It's such a pain," he said to Mom. "There were no elections at all while Yamamoto was here. My timing's always bad."

"Can't be helped," she said. Then, with a serious expression on her face she looked up from her magazine. "Do you think I've gained weight? It's all this food we keep being given! I'll have to exercise more, but there isn't even a pool here."

"There's the ocean just over there," said Dad. "But I suppose it's not that good for swimming, with all the fish feed floating around."

"Perhaps I'll start going to volleyball with Miki,"

Mom said with a smile. "Mr. Yoshida's very handsome. Miki, will you ask him if I can come along?"

"That's not funny!" said Dad. "You hear all the time about policemen's wives having affairs with local men. It wasn't while he was stationed here, but you know about Yamamoto's divorce. I don't want that happening to us."

"Well, what about you?" Mom replied with a sharp look. "How do I know you're not doing anything stupid?"

"Me? You've got to be kidding! There's all this stuff with the election and the kids shooting rockets at Toshiko-bā's house. It's wearing me out!"

To calm the feuding factions down, Dad thought up a compromise. Each side would choose two people to be arrested. Dad would arrest them under the Public Offices Election Law and put them in jail overnight. Both sides had said that arresting just one person wouldn't be enough—they were after a whole sweep. But the district had no jail, which meant that anybody he arrested would have to be taken to the town on the other side of the hills. If there were a lot of them, Dad would have to use a minibus, but there only were two vehicles like that in the village—one belonging to Marugi Fisheries, for taking staff to and from the plant, and the other to Abe Construction, for transporting workers to building sites. Under the circumstances, he couldn't very well borrow either.

So he decided to use his new Toyota Crown. The official patrol car had been another possibility, and, in the end, he regretted not using it, but he'd thought it would be overdoing things to use a patrol car in what was, after all, really just a mock arrest. Besides, if he was in his own car, he'd be able to go play pachinko afterward without attracting attention. So it seemed a good opportunity to take the new Toyota for a drive. He could only fit four people in the car besides himself, so that was why he settled on two detainees from each side. Mom told us that they were to be Iwaya and Hashimoto from Yoshi-nī's side and Hidaka and Someya from Hachi-nī's.

All four of them had been diagnosed with silicosis. Like Mitsugu Azamui and his hand-arm vibration syndrome, their diagnoses brought them a monthly government benefit, which meant they didn't have to work. Except for playing pachinko and chatting, none of them had anything in particular to do all day. In fact, they were perfectly happy to be arrested—they saw it as another way of supporting their candidates.

"It'll be good to see where the pigs put people," said Hidaka. "I know plenty about where people put pigs." His younger son had graduated from the prefecture's agricultural university and was now a pig farmer on the outskirts of the village.

Iwaya had two sons working as truck drivers at Marugi Fisheries, and Hashimoto's wife worked in the office. Before developing silicosis, Hidaka had for years been a manager at Abe Construction. Someya had originally been a fish-farmer. Everyone knew how his business had gone bankrupt before new techniques brought a boom to fish farming in the village. The story was a local legend. He blamed the fishing cooperative for refusing him financing, and of course the chairman of the cooperative, then as now, was Yoshi-nī. But in fact, most people believed—and maybe deep down Someya did too—that Yoshi-nī had actually saved him from much bigger losses. Someya had been like an unsteady surfer, unable to mount a big slow wave curving gently into the bay. If he'd had financing to expand his business, his failure would have been on a truly disastrous scale.

Though their various circumstances meant they had different allegiances in the election, the four men got along well. They certainly enjoyed being as rude as possible about each other, and used the foulest language, even when children were around. But it was only a bit of theater. After all, they'd all been born in the same small village and had known each other their whole lives. They weren't suddenly going to start hating each other. Their friendship couldn't be switched off like a TV. But family relationships were more difficult. When things turned sour there was no way back. You could see that from Yoshi-nī and his sister, Hatsue. The four men all agreed on that uncomfortable fact.

They arrived very early in the morning. I was leaving for volleyball practice just before 7:30 when I heard voices. They were standing outside the house, chatting.

"Dad!" I shouted. "They're here!"

Dad appeared through the front door in a hurriedly pulled-on pair of track pants, his hair sticking up at the back of his head.

"You're very early, gentlemen," he said, easing down the ski-jump tufts of hair.

"Shenshei," said Iwaya, "we thought that if we're goin' to town maybe we could um…" He gestured—a turn of his right wrist.

"Huh?" Dad said, imitating the move. He was still sleepy.

"Pachinko, shenshei," said Someya. "Why don't we play some pachinko?"

"Ah! Pachinko!" Dad said happily. "Sounds good!"

Then Mom appeared.

"How about some tea?" she asked.

"Great!" they all said. "Thank you!" and trooped into the police office.

"If only we'd waited until we got to town to go to the pachinko place there," said Dad.

They'd gone to the pachinko parlor on the highway this side of the pass. Iwaya and Hidaka had both won 30,000 yen there the previous day and they swore it paid out better than the one in town. Someya agreed, without giving the matter much thought. It had just been remodeled after a change of ownership. "Places like that always give better odds," he'd said.

"I should have known we'd be taken for a ride," Dad groaned.

"People who forget the past repeat the past," said Mom coldly. "You shouldn't have gone at all."

Dad sat in red-faced silence.

When they'd come out of the pachinko place the sun was already down. The western fringes of the hills were turning from indigo to black.

"We should at least have left before dark," said Dad with a heavy sigh.

Keiji was keen to hear all about it. He'd often said he wanted to see the animals that came out along the road up in the hills at night. Mom had said we couldn't have pets because of Keiji's asthma—which was maybe why he was so interested in animals. He was always watching nature programs on TV or looking at books about animals.

"There are no lights on the road up there," said Dad. "It was pitch black."

"Must have been scary," said Keiji.

"Not really—there were five of us in the car—we were enjoying ourselves."

"But wasn't that part of the problem?"

"Yes," said Dad, glancing at Mom. "I wasn't thinking straight."

"And when you came out of the tunnel…"

"Yes. It was just after the tunnel. I saw a kind of flash in front of us."

"Their eyes?"

"Yes. There were deer on the road."

"I wish I could have seen them. I've never seen any in real life, never seen a monkey, never seen a boar. How many deer were there?"

"Three, I think. One of them was small."

"Did the big ones have antlers?"

"No."

"So, they were does, then. One of them must have been the little one's mother." Keiji was proud of his knowledge. "And that's when it happened?"

"Yeah. It was stupid. The other guys in the car all shouted when they saw the deer. 'Hit one, shenshei! Deer! Hit one!'"

"Mr. Hashimoto said he'd hit one before, right?"

"Yeah, I think so. He hit it, kept the meat, and ate

it. But just then—in the car—we'd been talking about a boar."

Keiji looked astonished.

"Somebody hit a boar? Who?"

"Didn't I tell you? It was Ken, the guy who runs the Bungo Strait guesthouse—you know him, he sometimes brings us fish. He saw a boar on the road one day and thought to himself, 'A bit of stew would be good,' and drove straight at it. The car hit it hard, and the boar flew up into the air and landed in a heap on the road. But it wasn't dead. It was only pretending. It lay there, waiting for Ken to get out of the car and walk over. Then it jumped up, ran straight at him, knocked him over, and pinned him to the ground. The boar's front trotters were on his chest and he couldn't move. It was so heavy he could hardly breathe. The boar was snorting angrily through its nostrils and Ken thought he was going to be eaten, but he was saved at the last moment. Just as he'd given up all hope, a car came by. When the boar saw the car, it calmly walked off toward the hills. As it was leaving the road, it turned around, looked Ken straight in the eye, and gave a scornful smile. Then it disappeared. When Ken got back to the car, he saw there was a terrible dent in the front. And he was covered in fleas from the boar. He was scratching himself for days!"

"Boars aren't carnivores, Dad," Keiji corrected him with a momentary frown. "And I wonder if they really smile." His eyes were now sparkling with curiosity.

"Well…" said Dad, with a shrug. "But anyway, they coaxed me into it with their shouting: 'Hit it! Hit it!' I shouldn't have listened. I suppose I must have been thinking: *It's not a boar; it's a deer. It won't cause any damage...* And there were no other vehicles around. 'Hit it! Hit it!' they kept shouting and before I knew what I was doing I had the accelerator flat to the floor. Then there was a terrible noise and I slammed on the break. As soon as we stopped, everyone jumped out of the car and there was something lying on the road.

"But it wasn't dead, was it?"

"No. When we got close it hopped up and ran off."

"After being hit by a car...amazing!"

It was the second time Keiji had heard the story, but he looked just as surprised as he had the first time.

"Yeah," said Dad. "Then we went back to the car. It was in a hell of a state. The bumper was bent, the left headlight was broken, and there was a dent in the hood. The other four were laughing their heads off. 'The deer was tougher than the car,' they said. Well, all I could do was laugh along with them, though really there was nothing to laugh about." He smiled sadly.

"Nothing at all," said Mom sternly from the kitchen.

"Deer must be really strong!" said Keiji, trying not to snicker.

But they're not. At least, they're no match for a car.

As usual, Mitsugu Azamui was already drunk when he arrived at the house that day. What was different this time was that Dad was pretty drunk too. He and Mom had been arguing a lot about the car, and of course he always came off worst, so his confidence was at a low ebb. Mom was away for the night, on a trip to the Dogo Onsen hot spring, organized by the women's association.

The trip had been proposed by Hatsue, the deputy

chair. The election had gone very well as far as Hatsue was concerned. Her husband, Hachi-nī, was now a member of the district assembly, and although her brother, Yoshi-nī, had retained his seat, his ranking had fallen. Until then he had always gotten the most votes of any candidate in the whole district, but Hachi-nī had successfully eaten into his support in the village. Hachi-nī's own share of the vote was not huge—the second lowest of the successful candidates—but he'd gotten his seat. Mr. Kawano had done better than expected this time around, attracting the most votes of any of the defeated candidates. But, of course, defeat was still defeat.

Hatsue was delighted by her husband's success.

"We couldn't have done it without shenshei and you," she told Mom, urging her to come on the trip. Hatsue (or rather Abe Construction) paid for Mom's expenses, as well as those of several other women who had contributed to the Hachi-nī cause.

Because Mom was away, I had to serve drinks for Dad and Mitsugu Azamui. Well, I didn't *have* to, exactly, but Dad was very down because of the car and it seemed like a nice thing to do. We had the curry that Mom had left us, and then I quietly took him a glass. It seemed to cheer him up.

"Would you like some fries?" I said.

"Sure!" he said, nodding happily.

I'd bought some frozen fries that afternoon and I put them in the microwave. Keiji stood next to me, drooling.

"Aren't they ready yet?" he demanded impatiently, peering through the glass.

It wasn't long before the microwave went *ping*, but at that very same moment we heard a voice from the veranda.

"Evening!"

It was Mitsugu Azamui. Keiji's face fell.

"Save some for me!" he said, almost in tears. "I'll be in my room. Bring me some up there!"

Dad was drinking more quickly than usual. He and Mitsugu were in the living room as always, and I was watching from the kitchen. It wasn't that easy to tell who was who. Dad was slouching forward just like Mitsugu. It looked as if only the table was keeping him from sinking away altogether. Mitsugu Azamui was even thinner than he had been on his previous visit. His drooping head looked oddly large on his small body. His face, tarnished by sun and alcohol, was almost the same color as his dull, close-shaved hair. His eyes looked like wounds gouged into his flat face. They oozed a yellow discharge. His whole head was like a rotten fruit that might at any moment topple onto the table.

"You had some bad luck, shenshei," said Mitsugu, staring straight at Dad. His voice was strangely harsh and dry, as though the alcohol had burned his throat. Normally Mitsugu would have to make an effort to lift his eyes when looking at Dad, as though turning heavy stones. But today Dad's face was so low that Mitsugu didn't have to move a muscle.

"Damaged your new car?"

"Yeah. I'm ashamed of myself," groaned Dad. "It's

a real headache. I'd only just bought it."

"Were you really tryin' to kill a deer?" asked Mitsugu. He was still staring straight at Dad. Once fixed on something, his dull, cloudy eyes didn't shift easily. It was these eyes that frightened Keiji the most.

"Yeah. They all encouraged me—Hidaka and the rest. 'Hit it! Hit it!' they said, so I…"

"Was it really a deer?"

"What?"

"The thing you hit. Was it really a deer?"

I didn't know what he meant. Dad looked confused. He didn't seem to know what to say. "Were you watching?" he said eventually.

Mitsugu didn't speak right away. His gaze was still fixed on Dad. Something stirred in his dull eyes, but it couldn't gather enough force to break free. It stayed where it was, shifting uncertainly.

"Toshiko-bā always says she wants to die," Mitsugu murmured, forcing each word out painfully. "'I wanna die, I wanna die!' she says."

Again, Dad didn't seem to know how to respond. Why were they suddenly talking about Toshiko-bā? "Has something happened to her?" Dad said dubiously.

"She's always sayin' she wants to die… You sure it wasn't her on the road, shenshei? Wasn't she lyin' in the road like before?" He paused breathlessly between each question. "Was it really a deer you hit, shenshei? Or was it Toshiko-bā?"

"Yamamoto said something about someone lying in the road once, didn't he?" said Dad, glancing toward me in the kitchen.

When Mr. Yamamoto was the policeman here, someone had come knocking on his door early one morning. It was a young truck driver from Marugi Fisheries. He told Mr. Yamamoto that there was an old woman lying on the road and he couldn't get his truck around her. He wanted Mr. Yamamoto to do something about it. The truck driver had tried his best to get her to move, but she simply wouldn't. It was all very strange. If it had been a drunk, then maybe it wouldn't have seemed so odd, but it was an old woman. There weren't even any houses nearby. It was such a peculiar situation that the driver couldn't bring himself to pull her off the road, but no matter what he said to her, she just lay there, stock-still, eyes closed. He'd begun to worry that he might have hit her somehow without realizing. But then, to his relief, he noticed some faint movement in her throat. Seeing that she was alive, he turned his truck around and went to Mr. Yamamoto's house for help.

Mr. Yamamoto told Dad that the driver had described the old woman's face as rough and craggy. Mr. Yamamoto went back with the driver, but when they got to where he'd seen her, there was nobody there. No sign of her at all.

"The driver looked stunned," Mr. Yamamoto said. "As though he'd been tricked by a spirit. 'I saw her right there,' he'd said, pointing at the road. Maybe I should have checked if he'd been driving drunk," he laughed. "Anyway, it's a strange place." He tapped Dad on the shoulder. "Be careful *you* don't get tricked by any spirits while you're there."

Dad was looking at me.

"I wonder if that old woman was Toshiko-bā."

Of course, I didn't know.

"Toshiko-bā always says she wants to die," said Mitsugu Azamui again. "You sure it was a deer you hit, shenshei?"

Toshiko-bā was another big name in the village. The kids, especially, were scared of her.

Mitsugu Azamui's stare was certainly unnerving—his eyes always looked as though they were about to slip out of their sockets. But his drunkenness matched a familiar stereotype and, in its way, seemed almost comical.

His specialty was passing out at people's houses, or sometimes on the side of the road. Ken from the Bungo Strait guesthouse once decided to carry him home. He began to regret his kindness when he felt warm liquid running down his back.

"Piss! It was piss! Mitsugu Azamui wet himself on my back! Ugh!"

Ken's story was met with an explosion of laughter, like a toilet blowing off its lid.

Dad swore he'd never carry Mitsugu home, even if he fell asleep at our house.

"But then he might wet himself here," Keiji said, looking anxiously up at Dad.

"Hmm…I suppose he might. That wouldn't be too good, would it?"

Dad and Keiji looked at each other and laughed.

But even when Mitsugu did fall asleep at our house it was never necessary for Dad to carry him home. All

he had to do was call Mr. Kawano. It was a small village and Mr. Kawano would arrive within five minutes.
Even if Dad didn't call, Mr. Kawano seemed to have
an instinct as to where Mitsugu would be and he'd often simply turn up to collect him just after eleven. Mr.
Kawano always looked sad when he arrived. Mitsugu
was a struggle to handle—his body would bend this
way and that as if it had extra joints. In his drunken
state, Mitsugu seemed to forget he was a human being,
forget that he could walk on two legs. Fortunately, he
lived nearby and Mr. Kawano always managed to get
him home.

I feel uncomfortable saying this and perhaps out of respect for Mr. Kawano, I shouldn't, but to the bystander,
Mitsugu Azamui's drinking wasn't that terrible. As he
tried to drink himself from humanity back into an
inorganic state, he never became argumentative or violent. He even had a certain charm. People may have
ridiculed or pitied him, they may have shaken their
heads and sighed, but they still smiled. But when it
came to Toshiko-bā there was nothing whatsoever to
smile about.

Almost all the junior high boys fired bottle rockets
at her house. It was their obsession, but not even they
seemed to know why they did it.

"I did it when I was at junior high, too," said Mr.
Yoshida, as if it were inevitable. "I don't know why. I
suppose because the older boys did. Everyone did it
back then, just like now."

The only boy in the school who didn't fire rockets at Toshiko-bā's house was Shiotsuki Toshikazu.

He played first base and batted sixth in baseball—but then, there were only forty kids in each grade. All the boys played baseball and all the girls played volleyball.

He was a head and a half taller than the rest of the class and much heavier too. In winter, when there was no baseball, the school entered him in the district sumo tournament, and he won it. He went on to be runner-up at county level and then reached the semifinals of the prefectural tournament, getting his photo in the local papers. Apparently, scouts had come to watch him—not just from a high school with a strong sumo team, but from professional sumo stables as well.

But Toshi's real love was baseball. His problem was he couldn't remember the signs, and when he tried to steal a base without the sign he always got out. He was the slowest runner in the class. Once, when having gotten a double, he heard the defenders shouting, "Two out, two out, concentrate!" He joined in, sticking his hand in the air with his thumb and little finger raised, and shouted, "Two out, two out, keep tight!" Both teams burst out laughing, as did the umpire, and the game ground to a halt for a while.

He lived with his father and younger brother. He'd recently lost his granny, Mitsu. She wasn't his real grandmother, he told me, but she'd always played that role in the family. She'd been given an impressive send-off at the community hall, thanks to the Abes—Hatsue and Hachi-nī. Hatsue had organized the food, there being no mother in the household. The community hall was just across the road from the police office so we could hear the impressive voice of Tahara, the priest, as he chanted sutras.

Tahara was another regular visitor to our house. When he was drunk he always moaned, making every-body uncomfortable. He'd go on and on about how his hair was thinning, even though his job meant he had to shave his head bald anyway. He'd grumble about get-ting fat because of all the food people gave him when he performed ceremonies for them. He complained about how his new stole ruined his look because it kept sliding off his shoulder. He'd sit in our living room with his seventh whisky on the rocks and whine endlessly about anything to do with his appearance. He obvi-ously cared a lot about it. His eyebrows were always carefully plucked. Apparently, he'd bought some special Italian tweezers at Sony Plaza in Osaka after a trip to his sect's head temple in Kyoto. Mom looked at herself in her hand mirror when she heard about that.

"I'm so jealous," she said to Dad, who was sprawl-ing on the floor. "Those are exactly what I want! Any chance of you getting sent on a trip to Osaka?"

"Why would an Oita policeman be sent to Osaka?" said Dad, bemused. "They have nothing in common but the character *O*!"

Toward evening the villagers would come outside to enjoy the cool air on the main road by the bay. The onshore wind blew wearily toward them, while the bay, holding tight to the smell of the sea, waited pa-tiently for night. The police house was at the junction of the main street and a small side road, so people of-ten stopped in front of our garden to chat with each other. The men who'd guided Dad's car toward disas-ter—Hashimoto, Hidaka, Someya, and Iwaya, along with Iwaya's dog, Shiro—gathered frequently and often talked for a very long time.

Dad had begun to call them the Silica Four, a name he'd picked up from Mr. Kawano. Mr. Kawano had no sympathy for them at all, regarding them as living lazy lives at tax-payers' expense. At the same time, they were all former students of his, so he seemed to feel some responsibility for how they'd turned out. Whenever he saw them, he'd stop his bicycle, walk over, and say something like:

"Is this what my teaching's done?"

Then he'd stand, gazing at them mournfully, shaking his head for a full three minutes. The four of them would exchange embarrassed glances, laughing with exaggerated cheeriness. Even Shiro would seem embarrassed, looking up at Mr. Kawano, his tail between his legs, his front paws over his nose.

But Mr. Kawano's greatest sadness was Mitsugu Azamui. Mr. Kawano had raised him. Nobody in the village seemed to know about Mitsugu's birth, but they all knew that, as a young couple, Mr. Kawano and his wife had taken him in. And the child they'd nurtured with all their care had ended up an alcoholic, living off benefits for what may or may not have been a genuine case of hand-arm vibration syndrome. In a sense, Mitsugu Azamui was, in human form, the antithesis of the capitalist society that Mr. Kawano hated—the end point of his criticism of that whole social system. But I don't think this made him happy in the least. When he looked at Mitsugu Azamui, Mr. Kawano's eyes were filled with pain.

Mrs. Kawano—Kimie—had died some years before.

People said she'd worried about Mitsugu until the very end. But Mitsugu, himself abandoned by his wife and children, had long since abandoned his adoptive parents. He never once visited Kimie in the hospital.

But Mr. Kawano had never abandoned Mitsugu. Whether he lay drunk at the side of the road or at our house, it was Mr. Kawano who carried him home. Mr. Kawano always looked so sad as he was doing it.

But whenever any of the Silica Four saw Mr. Kawano carrying Mitsugu, they felt relieved.

"At least we ain't as bad as Mitsugu!" they'd say. "Dunno how shenshei copes!"

Tahara the priest had been in the same grade as the Silica Four at school and even now he was still a target of their mockery.

"That priest's a wuss, ain't he," said Iwaya one time when he ran into the other three on his way back from a walk with Shiro.

"Lucky you've got Shiro to protect you." They all laughed.

"He always was a bit of a girl," said Someya, adjusting his false teeth.

"But he sounds like a man all right when he's chanting his sutras," said Hashimoto with genuine enthusiasm. "*Kaaa-ttsu!*"

Hashimoto's sudden shout in imitation of the priest boomed across the bay. Shiro barked in approval, wagging his tail happily. The Silica Four laughed, as though they were being tickled by Shiro's fluffy tail.

Shiotsuki Takeo, my classmate Toshi's father, had worked for a while as a marine crane operator for Abe

Construction. While he was there, the event occurred that destroyed the relationship between Hatsue and her brother, Yoshi-nī. Takeo took responsibility for it and quit the company. He went back to fishing, the job he'd had before. Toshi helped his father with the catch and was often late for school—sharks are brought in before dawn, so after helping with that he'd go home to rest before school and almost inevitably oversleep.

Hatsue always did a lot for Toshi's family. The lunches that he and his brother brought to sports days and on field trips were all prepared by Hatsue. Mom said it must have been because Hatsue and Hachi-nī felt uncomfortable about firing Toshi's dad, which they'd done under pressure from Yoshi-nī. Toshi's dad was even taller than Toshi and had the build of a professional wrestler. He had a nice smile and seemed kind, but according to Mom he turned nasty when he drank. Things got so bad that Toshi's mom eventually left. It's difficult to judge people by appearances.

"But with your dad, what you see is what you get," she said, as Dad lay snoring on the tatami in his longjohns. His hairy calves looked repulsive.

Toshi's father didn't stop hitting his sons when his wife left. When Toshi was changing for P.E. his chubby back and shoulders were always covered in bruises. (There were no changing rooms—boys used the classrooms to change and girls the music room.) Sometimes he came to school with a swollen cheek or a black, bloodshot eye. On days like that he would sit at his desk all day and not talk to anyone, his face hidden behind his bulky arms. But he never missed school or after-school activities.

According to Hatsue, it was Toshi's mom that was in the wrong.

"She had another man," Hatsue said, curling her lip. "She started seeing him when she was working in a bar in town and then ran off with him to Kokura. But apparently he's now left her and she's back working at another bar." Hatsue proudly named the source of this latest information.

Toshi had no idea why his classmates fired rockets at Toshiko-bā's house. He shook his head, baffled, just like when he saw a sign he couldn't understand from the bench in baseball.

"Where's the fun in that? It'd be terrible for her if she was injured. What if she gets burned? If she gets any more burns, she'll die!"

But then, perhaps it was because of her burns that they fired the rockets. She was ugly. Her skin was like charred meat. Her face was rough and disfigured—as though a stream of lava had run over it, mixing with her blood and flesh and then solidifying. She was bald and had no eyebrows. There was a lump on her forehead, hanging down over her left eye. Some of her fingertips were missing, as if they'd melted away.

Neither I nor any of my classmates knew whether her scars were really burns or not. There was plenty of speculation. One of my friends said they were from an unidentifiable and incurable illness. "Contagious," she said. "If you caught it, you'd end up looking like her. Scary, right!" When that rumor started flying around, firework sales at Nakamoto's near the school shot up. Toshiko-bā's house was bombarded with arrows of bright flame, engulfed with deafening bangs and the smell of burning. There were beautiful patterns in the sky. Mr. Kawano flew into a rage. He grabbed a garden scythe and a hammer, rushed outside, and chased after the boys who were causing the trouble. "Stop! Stay right where you are, you little bastards!"

Some of the boys set off fireworks just for the thrill of being chased by Mr. Kawano. They wanted to provoke him. When he got close, they all ran away as fast as they could. "Here he comes!" they shouted. "Scythe-man! Aaahh!"

From that point of view, Mr. Kawano's concern for Toshiko-bā was having the reverse effect from what he intended. The more energetically he campaigned against the stupidity of firing rockets at her house, the more rockets went flying in.

Toshiko-bā walked bent over, one hand pressed against her stomach. Her other hand stretched out to the side as if feeling for an invisible handrail. She couldn't bend her right knee, so her right foot dragged along the ground. A lot of the boys imitated Mitsugu Azamui's drunkenness; but none of them imitated Toshiko-bā's strange walk.

It was painful to look at her. Little children were so frightened they cried when they saw her. The women disapproved of the boys firing rockets at her house, but they didn't want to get too close to it themselves. It was Mr. Kawano, living just opposite, who normally cleared up the debris, but if he managed to catch any of the boys, he made them do it. He'd stand behind them as they crouched to pick up the spent fireworks. They'd hear the sharp, dry sound of the scythe blade scratching against the hammer.

Of course, I didn't fire any rockets at Toshiko-bā's house, but that doesn't mean I felt any differently about her than the boys did. Whenever I saw her, I immediately looked away. Her appearance aroused a strange fear in people.

The only person who had regular contact with her was Mr. Kawano. Apparently, Yoshi-nī and his sister, Hatsue, were related to her somehow. But they never went near her house. Mr. Kawano, though, was sometimes seen going in with a pan of food.

To the villagers, Mr. Kawano was an oddball. They laughed at his obstinate string of election defeats, his campaign demands for better treatment of Toshiko-bā, and his rebukes of the children for moral depravity. Yet there was a softness and warmth in their laughter. They must have had a certain respect for him. Otherwise, he wouldn't have gotten any votes at all.

"He never got to be headmaster, but he was a good teacher," said Hidaka.

As usual, the Silica Four were chatting in front of the police office. Ken was with them.

"You're right. Best we ever had," said Hashimoto with a decisive nod.

"Without him and us, you'd never even have

graduated!" said Hidaka.

Everyone but Hashimoto laughed.

"Your attendance record was so bad they wouldn't have given you your diploma," said Iwaya. "Mr. Kawano had to come and ask our families if some of our days could be transferred to you." He smiled nostalgically.

Hashimoto had lived at a charcoal kiln in the hills, helping his father with his timber business. He'd very seldom come to school at all.

"Yeah, I remember," said Ken. "When he came to our house, my great uncle was there—Hide-jī."

Hide-jī had once been in the Imperial Guard. Everyone knew it was an honor to work at the Imperial Palace, so when he was leaving for Tokyo, the whole village gathered to see him off. Hide-jī sat straight-backed on his horse as he surveyed the assembled relatives and villagers. Finally, his eyes rested on his younger brother, Keisuke.

"Dear friends," he declared, "I shall now depart for the capital. From this day forth my brother Keisuke shall be head of the family. Kei, I entrust all matters entirely to you." And with that, he took his gallant leave.

He'd cut such a fine figure that it had become the stuff of village legend. Children were forever declaiming that the time had come for them to "depart for the capital."

Hide-jī had lost his wife and had no children, so in retirement he came to live with Keisuke and family. He used his savings to start, with Keisuke, the Bungo Strait guesthouse.

"Guess what he said when Mr. Kawano came to ask about the transfer and bowed down to him, hands on the floor?" said Ken. "It must have reminded him of the old days, when everyone showed him that kind of respect."

"What did he say, Ken?"

Ken straightened his back in the style of his great uncle and bowed his head:

"Gentlemen, I entrust the matter entirely to you."

Everyone laughed.

"Without those extra days, you'd have had to leave without a diploma," said Hidaka. "Mr. Kawano should be getting your vote at every election!"

Hashimoto said nothing. His face turned as red as a piece of high-grade charcoal hurled into a blazing fire.

The normal Mitsugu Azamui wasn't there that night—the man who drank in almost total silence. The Mitsugu Azamui in our house that evening was talking. His eyes were on Dad, but it was as if he didn't recognize that Dad existed. Was he looking at his own reflection in Dad's eyes and talking to himself? I don't think so. He was just talking. As if he himself didn't exist either. As if the only things that existed were the words.

Dad, like me, wanted to know why Toshiko-bā was how she was. I think that somehow, we were both waiting for somebody to explain. Dad listened in silence. I could only see his back; it looked different than normal—more tense.

This is the story Mitsugu told:

Toshiko-bā was Yoshi-nī's and Hatsue's aunt, their mother's younger sister. Their mother, Kiku, died long ago. Kiku was the oldest child in a large family and Toshiko the youngest, so they were very different ages, and when Kiku married the oldest son of the Todaka family, Toshiko was still small. Their parents were delighted that Kiku was marrying one of the Todakas, who controlled the village's fishing. Kiku's maiden name was Azamui. There were a lot of Azamuis in the village, many of them relatives, but none of them had their own businesses. Even by village standards they were poor.

Kiku wanted to help Toshiko go to middle school, an opportunity that Kiku herself had never had. But she was busy with her own two children and had to look after her aging father-in-law as well, so she couldn't think too much about her little sister. And her parents simply wanted her to do her best for her new family.

"Toshiko's a smart girl," her father said. "She'll be okay. Don't worry about her."

In fact, it turned out that the flow of support was more the other way, with Toshiko frequently coming over to the Todaka house to help Kiku. She was good at looking after the children.

It was the 1940s and the country was at war, but the conflict didn't stop the flow of migrants from the village to Japanese-controlled Manchuria. Toshiko was one of them. She had an uncle who was living in Harbin's new central district. He looked after the garden of a senior officer in Japan's Kwantung Army and had written to say that the colonel's household was looking for a maid.

Of course, Mitsugu didn't know firsthand what happened to Toshiko-bā in Manchuria. All he could do was repeat what other villagers who had been in Manchuria at the same time had told him. He couldn't tell whether her "reputation" was based on fact or not—it was only Toshiko-bā herself who knew the truth.

"It was the usual kind of thing," Mitsugu said, taking a sip from his glass with his eyes still on Dad. The hand clutching the glass was trembling as usual. He pressed the rim firmly against his mouth to prevent spillage, but a transparent vein of fluid still ran down his chin and dripped onto the table.

Toshiko wasn't beautiful, but she was a pleasant girl and her new employers took to her right away. There were just the two of them: the colonel, who worked at Kwantung Army Headquarters, and his wife. They had recently lost their seven-year-old daughter to typhoid. The colonel was busy with his work and he left all household matters to his wife. Their daughter had died very quickly. The colonel seemed to be silently blaming his wife, and the atmosphere in the house was uncomfortable. Perhaps because of their strained relationship, or because they were trying to see in Toshiko something of what their daughter might have become, both of them were very kind to her.

The colonel was especially fond of her. Unless he was eating or sleeping, almost all his time at home was spent in his study. When Toshiko took him tea, he'd be sitting in an armchair, looking out at the garden. He stroked the ends of his neatly trimmed mustache, seemingly lost in thought. Not turning around, he gestured to her to come closer. Without hesitation, she went and stood beside him. The colonel told her to sit on his knee. He spoke firmly and Toshiko did as she was told.

The colonel's thighs were thick and hard. His mustache bristled happily.

He stroked Toshiko's head. She glanced up and saw that he was still looking out at the garden.

In the garden was a row of stone lanterns that had been brought from Japan. There was even a tsukiyama mound. Toshiko didn't know she was looking at a Japanese-style garden. How could she? There was no garden as big as that in the village. Everything about it was entirely unfamiliar. As if to hide the house, a row of silver birch trees had been planted along the boundary wall. Every one of them was taller than any of the pines that grew in the hills behind the village. Their leaves were a thick green fog. They swayed and jostled in the strong wind. The noise of the street didn't penetrate. From somewhere in the garden she heard her uncle's voice, shouting at one of his young Chinese or Korean assistants. It startled her. She began to shake. She felt ashamed. Something was wrong. The colonel didn't seem to notice. He was entirely calm. She no longer knew what she was feeling. The colonel stroked her.

Her uncle was pleased. When Toshiko came to work at the house, he'd gotten a raise. And that wasn't all—the colonel gave her Japanese liquor and sweets to take home. They were all high-quality—brands that her uncle had never tasted before. On her way home, the neighborhood children would gather around her and ask what she'd been given that day.

When the colonel said he'd like her to live at the house, her uncle naturally had no objection. The colonel's wife was pregnant and had gone to her parents' house in Kyoto. With the happy news of his wife's pregnancy, Toshiko's uncle hoped the colonel might be even more generous.

The colonel applied himself to his work with still greater intensity. Perhaps the hope of another child gave him happiness and strength. He got home late, often eating out. He hardly ate at all in the mornings. He was making more frequent visits to a facility on the outskirts of Harbin. He only came home to sleep. Toshiko was on her own in the big house, but she didn't look forward to the colonel's return. She didn't feel that way at all. Every night before going to bed, he called her to his room. He'd get her to sit on his knee and he'd stroke her head. No matter how late it was, even when there was nothing outside but darkness, he would still look out toward the garden.

Toshiko had noticed the colonel gave off a peculiar smell. It was as though medicine—not traditional medicine, but chemical medicine—had seeped into the life held within his flesh. The sharp odor of chemicals didn't suppress the smell of flesh. Far from it. The smells seemed to combine in a stench of putrefaction. The chemicals had become a poison, a poison that putrefied things and that putrefied itself. It was a smell that shouldn't have existed. Perhaps it was this smell that made her so uneasy.

Her uncle came to the garden twice a week.

He'd put his head through the kitchen doorway, and leaving his assistants outside, come in. Toshiko felt uncomfortable letting someone into the house without permission, but her uncle said the colonel wouldn't mind. *I suppose not…* thought Toshiko. It was lonely eating on her own in the big house, so whenever her uncle came they had lunch together. "Boil up plenty of rice," he'd say. The tick of the grandfather clock next to the fireplace was like the heartbeat of the house, sounding through its cavernous spaces. The clock often stopped. Toshiko would suddenly notice the silence. The silence seemed to sneak around behind their backs as they ate, making its way out into the garden. Toshiko always prepared a little extra food and gave it to her uncle's young workers. He seemed to want her to. The young men talked wordlessly with the silence that came out of the house. When she gave them the food they stopped talking to the silence and ate. Her uncle probed his teeth with a toothpick and said nothing. He seemed happy watching them enjoy the rice.

One night, the colonel came home especially late. He'd left early that morning for yet another visit to the facility on the outskirts of the city. He seemed very tired. Perhaps that was why the smell seemed so strong. Tomoko shivered at the prospect of sitting on his knee. She didn't want to get close to him at all if she could help it.

But the colonel, looking out toward the invisible garden, called for her as he always did. The grandfather clock had stopped. She must have forgotten to wind it. Silence was pacing restlessly up and down the corridor.

"Yes," she said, and sat on the colonel's knee. He sighed. His neat mustache quivered. She grimaced at his breath. It stank like rotten meat. Something was rotting in the colonel's body. Maybe that something hadn't seeped in from outside. Maybe it had always been inside.

The colonel stroked Toshiko gently. He stroked and caressed her as if she were a pain tormenting his own flesh. The more he stroked the surface of her body the more she felt his poison get inside her. Perhaps there'd been poison in her already. Perhaps her poison and the colonel's poison were calling to each other. Seeping into her veins, mixing with her blood the poison was circulating through every part her body. The poisoned blood would build up and putrefy the flesh. The poison had to be removed before it was too late. The colonel must have realized that. Their bodies would have to be cut open and the blood removed. The colonel stroked Toshiko. He entered her. She let out a cry. But the blood that should have come didn't.

The colonel searched in the darkness for the blood that should have been there. He felt the wetness at the top of her thigh and lifted his hand to his eyes, but there was no blood. He ran his fingers back and forth over her, but saw no blood. Now he was certain, and he made his disappointment very clear. His normal composure gave way to intense rage. The poison was still inside her. She would have to live her life holding that poison inside. It made her very sad. Instead of the blood and poison that couldn't, tears flowed.

Yes. That was the problem. No blood.

"I have to speak to Mr. Yoshida," Dad said out of the blue.

Keiji and I were watching TV in the living room. The way he said it irritated me. He wasn't looking at me, and it was obvious he was trying to say it as if it didn't matter much. I looked at him, and just like when Mom made a sarcastic remark about the car, he dropped his gaze to the newspaper. I hated that about him. He looked like a frightened little dog that's waiting for someone to pet it. If it sees a stranger, it doesn't bite, doesn't even bark, it just watches nervously from a distance. It's not even sure if it should watch. And when it does, it wishes it hadn't.

Because of the boat that had suddenly appeared in the bay, Mr. Yoshida and I couldn't go to the tip of the promontory for a while. We couldn't go to the Marugi Fisheries office either. The boat's sudden arrival, and the fact that it didn't move on, made the villagers uneasy.

It was a battered old fishing boat—quite a large one—big enough for trips of a month or so to catch, say, yellowtail fry. What troubled the villagers most about it was the name that was crudely inscribed on the hull.

The boat was quite clearly the Midori Maru 18, which belonged to the Todaka family. The Midori Maru had left the bay many years before and hadn't been seen since. There was no mistaking the boat because the character 緑 (*midori* green) had been mistakenly written as 縁 (*en* connection), and despite all

48

the time that had passed, despite all the waves that must have crashed against the boat's hull, the thick black characters remained entirely legible, like a memory that never fades.

As he looked out at the boat in the bay, Mr. Kawano felt a rush of nostalgia, along with a twinge of embarrassment. The boat had been built by his father—a carpenter and joiner, who, on occasion, had been called upon to deal with broken bones and sprained joints. It was he who had made the mistake with the name, providing the other villagers with considerable amusement. Not long afterward, the Kawano family left for Manchuria. They'd been planning to go anyway, but some of the villagers felt guilty that their departure might have been hastened by the persistent teasing.

One clear consequence of the error was the younger Kawano's eventual career. Kawano senior didn't want him to suffer any similar humiliations, so he resolved that his son should go to college, which led him into teaching. So, you could say that if it hadn't been for the boat, the young Kawano Itaru would never have become the village's "Mr. Kawano." Before that, though, the incident led him to turn his back on love and concentrate on his studies.

The young Kawano Itaru's first love was Todaka Hatsue, whose father ordered the boat. These days Hatsue is overweight and far from good-looking, but apparently she was quite attractive when she was young.

"Even bulldogs are cute when they're puppies," said Iwaya.

Iwaya loved dogs. His own Akita mutt, Shiro, was fond of people and had never bitten anyone. Iwaya never tied him up; Shiro wouldn't have minded if he had. Shiro was lazy, and except when on a walk with Iwaya, he spent all day lying in the yard. Even cats cast him disdainful looks as they passed by. He lay asleep in the sunshine with his slobbery tongue lolling from his mouth. Just like his owner, people said. When Iwaya took him for walks in the hills, he often got caught in the snares that Iwaya set for wild boar. And then Iwaya would have to lug his heavy dog home, with it yelping the whole way. We could always hear Iwaya shouting as he struggled to loosen the snare. "You stupid animal! Do you mean to get snared?"

Hatsue was very angry about the mistake with the boat's name and was extremely rude to Kawano senior, using language people don't normally expect from a young girl. Her unkindness made young Kawano Itaru desolate. The romantic boy, the budding communist, had always imagined there was something wonderful inside this rather ordinary-looking girl— the colors of the rainbow, a shining milk-white pearl. But now foul water had gotten inside the shell. There was no point in opening it up. His feelings suddenly grew cold—like a morning fog descending on the bay.

To Hatsue, her furious outburst was entirely reasonable. The boat was very special to her. Her father had given her the honor of naming it, though he'd said it had to be the "eighteenth." Hatsue didn't know why, since it was actually the family's third boat. The second one had been the "eighth," so she guessed there must be some special reason.

"Eight's a lucky number," her father told her. "Because of the way the lines on the character 八 open out."

She was disappointed the explanation was so simple.

Until then it had been her brother, Yoshi, who had been allowed to name everything, not just boats, but their animals too: dogs, cats, goats, anything that merited a name. Hatsue had only ever named one animal, a sow which had forfeited its original name— Momo—for biting her brother on the butt. The pig had turned on him when he stuck a fire cracker in its anus and tried to light it. Nobody had asked Hatsue to give the disgraced pig a new name, but she decided she would call it "Midori," because of its greenish eyes. She looked after Midori every day.

When the boat was completed, there was a big celebration. Hatsue thought she'd give Midori some of the leftovers. Midori always had leftovers from the family's meals, but that day's leftovers were very special and, as she walked toward the barn, Hatsue imagined Midori's nose wriggling and twitching with pleasure. But when she got there, Midori wasn't anywhere to be found. Hatsue called and called, but Midori didn't come.

"Midori's not in the barn, Mom," said Hatsue, on the verge of tears.

Her mother was busy washing dishes by the well.

"Your pig's right there," said Yoshi.

Kiku, their mother, gave him a sharp look, but carried on washing.

Yoshi didn't stop. He didn't want to.

"It's right in front of your nose!"

"Where?" shouted Hatsue. She didn't want to believe it.

"In your hands!" said Yoshi, with a cruel smile.

Midori had been part of the feast and was now in the pile of leftovers on the plate in Hatsue's hands. But not just on the plate. She was in the guests' stomachs. In Yoshi's stomach. And, of course, in Hatsue's own stomach.

Seeing Hatsue so upset, her father hit Yoshi over the head and announced, much to his son's annoyance, that Hatsue could name the new boat.

Hatsue decided to call it "Midori Maru." To her, the boat had been given life through the sacrifice of Midori the pig. It was the reincarnation of Midori.

But then, after all that, Itaru's father made the mistake with the boat's name. Hatsue's father didn't seem bothered by it—"the characters don't look that different," he said. He didn't ask for it to be changed.

Yoshi was delighted by the mistake. He joined forces with his friend Abe Hachiro to mock Itaru, and they gathered a gang of little boys who followed them, parroting what they said.

For Hatsue there was no emotion but anger. She had gone around the entire village talking to people excitedly about the launch of the Midori Maru, all the time thinking of it as the rebirth of Midori. Her fury did not subside.

Mine didn't either.

"I'd better talk to Mr. Yoshida."

I'd heard Dad say that so often! And every single

time, he acted as though he was on a different wavelength from everyone else, as if the words were part of some interior monologue, a sentence that just happened to pop out of his mouth. It was totally unconvincing. What exactly was it he wanted to say to Mr. Yoshida? It was really getting on my nerves. I just wanted him to stop his ridiculous performance.

He stood with the newspaper and walked toward the door. I glared at him.

"What are you going to say to Mr. Yoshida?" I said.

Keiji shrank away at the tone of my voice. He watched me nervously. He looked exactly like Dad, which got my hackles up all the more.

"What's the matter with you?" I said, turning my aggression on him.

He looked back at the TV, trying to ignore me.

"What?" I shouted.

"So scary! Scarrrry!" said Dad, as though he had no idea why I was angry.

I glared at him again—a middle-aged personification of indecision, a caricature of a person whose primary aim in life is to avoid confrontation at all costs.

If he wanted to say something about me and Mr. Yoshida, I wanted him to say it straight out. Why did he have to leave it all as ambiguous insinuation? It was obvious what he was thinking. His eyes said it all.

"So scary! You on your period?" Dad said, hurriedly escaping into his office. "Save us, Buddha! Save us!"

So that was that. Typical. He didn't know a thing. No, I wasn't on my period. That was exactly the problem.

When I told Mr. Yoshida, he didn't say anything. He obviously didn't have the faintest idea what to do. It was dark in the car, but I saw a flash of regret cross his face, like a moment of moonlight on the night-black surface of the bay. I was disappointed. *It's hard for me too*, I almost said.

We sat in silence, looking at the boat as it floated alone in the bay. It hadn't moved at all. It was like a trace of something stranded between memory and oblivion. But I didn't know what that something was.

I'd slipped out of the house while the rest of the family was asleep. With all the fuss about the appearance of the ghost ship, workers were taking turns staying in the Marugi Fisheries building overnight, so we still couldn't use the office.

When Mr. Yoshida turned on the engine of his GTR Turbo it snarled, like some fierce animal warning off a foe. Whenever I got in to go with him to the tip of the promontory I was nervous it would wake the neighbors. I always sank as low as possible in my seat and kept my head down as we passed the plant so I wouldn't be seen.

Mitsugu Azamui walked right past us. Mr. Yoshida had parked the GTR on the road by the beach at the tip of the promontory. Mitsugu was walking alone along the shore. It seemed like he was always there late at night. From the side, his face was like a mask, a profile of the monarch of some lost realm, frozen in time. Sometimes when he came by, we'd be playing a CD or the radio, but he never looked toward the car. It was as though this profile was all that existed. What if that were true? *Don't look this way*, I muttered under my breath. There was a large bottle in his hand, like a scepter—the only thing that was faithful to this solitary king. The liquid was pure, transparent—reflecting the scepter's fidelity. But was it really pure? It was difficult to tell in the moonlight. The king was suspicious and, wanting to establish its true motivations, kept lifting it to his eye and looking deep within. Then he'd press it to his lips, as though the degree of fidelity would be revealed by the pleasure the liquid gave as it ran down his throat.

Mitsugu made no sound as he walked—a king abandoned even by his own footsteps. All that remained to him was his bottle scepter. The only sound was from the waves—perhaps it was the sea's song of solace for the king. The sea had nothing to fear from the king's harsh tongue. It was just an observer and could afford to be generous. Squeezed out from his body, Mitsugu's shadow stretched crazily across the bay in the clear light of the moon. It was like a searchlight looking for people in distress, though in fact it wasn't looking for anything. It was wanting to be found. It wavered on the surface of the water, sad and unstable.

In the end, the shadow searchlight found nothing in the bay but the ghost ship. I wondered how on earth Mitsugu Azamui could have found a body on the beach.

He'd mentioned the body when he told Dad about Toshiko-bā. But that was a long time after we'd first started seeing him at the beach.

Sometimes, after Mitsugu Azamui left the beach, Mr. Yoshida and I walked there too. We were curious about what he'd been doing, so we'd follow his footsteps. They always disappeared into the water. They headed for the sea, like a turtle after laying its eggs. Besides his footsteps, there was never anything else there. We never saw a body.

We did see something, though. It wasn't a body—more like a living person. I can't say definitely that it was a living person. It could have been a ghost. Mr. Yoshida didn't seem certain that he'd seen it at all.

"It won't make any difference now," said Mr. Yoshida.

My period was well overdue, and there were no signs of it coming. I was anxious and didn't want to do it at first. To tell the truth, I was disappointed by Mr. Yoshida's remark. He wasn't taking the matter seriously. It was only his fingers and tongue that showed any kind of sincerity. Like a climber on a precipice, every little movement was vital. Nothing was neglected. Before I knew it, I was just a sack of skin, swelling with a mush of anxiety and relief. The ground shook, equilibrium was lost, a rush of heat. The climbers could go no further. The mush broke through the surface of my body, spilling out. Mr. Yoshida frantically tried to plug the wound.

And after the ecstasy, a daze. Without really looking at anything, we stared out over the bay. The boat was there as always.

Strangely, nobody went near the boat.

Dad asked the Silica Four why the villagers all left it alone.

"No sense getting involved again in the argument between Yoshi-nī and Hachi-nī," Hidaka said.

"That's true," nodded the other three. Shiro, the dog, nodded too.

About a week earlier, Hatsue had come to our house in a very odd state of mind. She seemed half-crazed, like a fly buzzing around fish laid out to dry in the sun. "Something's happened!" she was yelling with tears in her eyes. "It's Midori Maru! Midori Maru's come back!"

Mom and Dad didn't know what to think. They had no idea what she was talking about. Mom poked Dad in the side and he hesitantly cleared his throat.

"Um, I'm sorry, Hatsue-san, but what exactly is Midori Maru?"

"My boat!" she said. "My boat! My boat! My boat!" she repeated, addressing each of us in turn. "It's come back. It disappeared when I was a kid, but now it's back!"

She sat down and Mom gave her some tea. While she drank it, we heard about how the boat had gotten its name.

Mr. Yoshida and I were looking over the bay.

It was a stifling night. We'd both been panting and sweating. The window was open, but there was no breeze coming through it. The sun had gone, but its heat remained. Normally a wind picked up over the bay when the sun went down, but there was no wind that night. It never brought much relief anyway. It was warm and damp and, as though already laden with human sweat, it left drops of salty water on our skin.

Even if there had been a wind, the sticky fluids that bound our bodies wouldn't have dried.

While we were at it, Mr. Yoshida felt under the steering wheel for the car key. He turned on the battery and pressed a button on the dashboard, switching on the radio by mistake. It was an AM broadcast with a lot of interference, but I could tell it was in a foreign language. We often picked up Korean or Chinese stations in the village. I'd heard them during the previous summer holiday when I was trying to tune in to English broadcasts from NHK for my homework. Sometimes I'd just sit there for a while, listening vacantly to the unknown sounds.

Mr. Yoshida switched the radio off and eventually found the air conditioning. He pressed a button to close the tinted windows. They rose steadily, like the sensation in my body. They reached the top and *zip*, they closed, as though sealing a tear in the atmosphere. Suddenly the car was unbearably hot. The AC had started to hum, but at first the air it blew out was hotter than our breath. It took hold of every inch of the car's interior. I felt suffocated, as if I was being squeezed into a plastic bag that had been out all day in the sun. I thought of the plastic insect box my brother had left lying by the veranda at home. The big desiccated-looking beetle inside was in constant motion, its convulsing wings battering relentlessly against the sides of the box. As though it had used up all the available air, it seemed desperate to hasten its own death. But it would dry out and die soon enough anyway—lie at the bottom of the cage, legs folded neatly like so many pocket knives. The death of a beer bottle cap—a moment of pressure, then tossed away.

Once the AC got going, the air in the car cooled quickly and when we were finished I began to feel cold. I told Mr. Yoshida and he turned off the AC and opened the windows. Hot air came rushing in—hordes of starving people swarming into a palace after the dictator has fled: forcing the great doors and, overrunning the palace, mad with anger and delight, grabbing riches that had originally been plundered from the people, from them. Mr. Yoshida and I had just finished plundering each other, but the heat was still in our bodies, and it answered the call of the waves of hot air sweeping in from outside. We were soon drenched in sweat again.

As we stared out over the dozing bay, letting the sweat flow, Mr. Yoshida turned on the car lights, illuminating the surface of the water. Maybe the light was too dazzling, but the water didn't look red or murky at all. It shone pure black in the darkness, the waves gently rising and falling. It looked pristine, unblemished. But it couldn't be. The sea was filthy.

The filth was painted over by the cosmetic of night. In the daytime the water stagnated, like a swamp. From the viscous green mud that lay in its depths, there emerged a giant red snake. It swam at will around the bay, its grimy, fat-encrusted scales glistening as the sun beat down like a rainstorm. The wind stopped when the red tide came. The huge snake, born of polluted water, feared that its delicate red coat might disintegrate in a cool wind, like the patterns in a sand dune. The village grew hot and humid, so hot that it was hard to breathe. There was a bad smell in the air near the bay—as if creatures were beginning to rot within their tightly closed shells.

The red tide didn't just bring the terrible windless heat. It was also one of the causes of the final breakdown of the relationship between Hatsue and Yoshi-nī.

"It was the red tide that did it," said Someya, as if to himself, hurriedly putting his hand to his mouth to keep his false teeth in place.

"Yeah," said Hidaka, "it was all the pollution. The assembly decided to do some dredging. Of course, it was Yoshi-nī's suggestion. He was deputy chair of the assembly, as well as head of the fishing co-op."

The reason for the frequent red tides in summer was all the fish feed that was put in the yellowtail pens. Everyone knew this, but they couldn't stop feeding the yellowtail. So, the sea was polluted, the water temperature had risen, and oxygen levels had fallen. This killed a lot of pearl oysters. And now you couldn't grow oysters as easily as before. The board of the fishing co-operative thought the reason for the rise in water temperature was that the water wasn't flowing as well as it used to. If the flow were improved there'd be no build-up of sludge, and the red tides would no longer happen. They thought that things were bound to improve if the sediment and rubbish that had accumulated on the seabed were cleared away. This was their conclusion, and the fishermen agreed.

Yoshi-nī pushed the assembly to take action. Though 70 percent of his company's profits came from dried fish, he was also involved in yellowtail and oyster farming. It was a problem that his company, Marugi

Fisheries, couldn't ignore. Once the assembly decided that the dredging would be undertaken as public works, the next question was which construction company would get the contract. The answer seemed so obvious there was hardly any point in putting it out for bids.

As everyone expected, Yoshi-nī proposed Abe Construction, run by his brother-in-law, Hachi-nī. The assembly chairman had no objection. The dredging had been Yoshi-nī's suggestion, so it wasn't for the chairman to interfere. If the red tides hurt Marugi Fisheries' profits, the district's tax revenues would be hit in turn. Marugi Fisheries was a very important tax contributor. The geography of the area, with its irregular ria coastline, made it difficult to attract investment, and Marugi Fisheries was effectively the district's sole industry. So, a problem for Marugi Fisheries was a problem for the whole district.

Yoshi-nī was a very talented man who'd taken what had been just a small fishing concern and turned it into one of the prefecture's leading seafood businesses. The fat man wouldn't be wrong. As the villagers said, he had his bodyweight in gold and confidence. They should just do what he said.

Hatsue was very pleased. Her brother was sending business her husband's way. Maybe he wasn't such a bad person after all. She might even try to forget the matter about Midori the pig. At the time, Toshi's father, Takeo, was working for Abe Construction as a marine crane operator. He'd be pleased too, she thought. The more hours he put in, the more he'd be paid. There couldn't be any dredging without a crane.

"You see, Hatsue was fond of Takeo," said Hashimoto.

"He's a good man when he don't drink, but…" said Someya, shaking his head sadly, his hand over his mouth.

"You can't judge by appearances," said Dad, watering the roses in the flower bed.

"When he drinks, he goes wild," said Iwaya. Shiro shivered. "Look, Shiro knows all about it. He was just a puppy when things got very bad."

Iwaya began to tell the story. His house was next door to the Shiotsukis'. Because of his silicosis payments he had a good income and had built a three-story house in reinforced concrete, covering almost his entire plot. The rest of the Silica Four had similar properties nearby, leading people to talk—half in envy, half in contempt—about their "Silicon Palaces" or the village's "Beverly Hills." The Shiotsukis' house was very small in comparison. It could almost have passed for an outbuilding of the Iwayas' house. It was a shabby-looking place, with tarred plank walls. There was no flush toilet—just a hole in the ground in a shed outside. It seemed almost unbelievable that there were four people living there, including a man of Takeo's size. Mrs. Shiotsuki—Machiko—was still with the family in those days. She just put up with her husband's violence. The first thing that he did when he got home every day was reach for a bottle of shochu. He drank it like water. If Machiko said something like, "It's not good for you to drink so much," he hit her.

"Don't fucking tell me what to do, bitch!"

Then if she shut her mouth, he hit her again:

"Don't fucking look at me like that!"

Toshi's little brother, Yukihiro, was six and would always start crying. His father would shout at him, threatening to hit him. When Machiko tried to protect the boy, she'd get hit again. Toshi, who was eleven, would stare at his father with utter hatred.

"Who the fuck do you think you are?" his father shouted, hurling a glass across the room.

Then, standing up, he grabbed Toshi by the neck, pushed him onto the floor, sat on top of him, and started to punch him. Toshi didn't make a sound. He closed his eyes tight, though he couldn't stop the tears slipping out from behind his eyelids. He clenched his teeth, determined not to let a murmur of pain or sorrow cross his lips. Machiko was delicately framed and smaller than her eleven-year-old son, but she pushed her husband with all her strength.

"Stop it!" she cried.

She managed to get Toshi free and stood in front of him, protecting him. Her husband's rage intensified.

"I'll teach you, you fucking bitch!" he roared and began hitting her wildly.

Tears flowed from her eyes. Blood flowed from her nose and mouth. Toshi's face was badly bruised and his forehead was bleeding from where it had been caught by his father's metal watchband. Worried by the uproar, Iwaya and his wife, Sachiko, rushed over from next door.

"That's enough! Come on, Takeo! That's enough!" said Iwaya. He tried to steady the big man's hand, but was pushed away.

Then Sachiko threw herself around his log-like arm and clung on tight.

"Take-chan, stop it! That's enough, Take-chan!"

She was talking to him as if he were a child, searching for the little Take-chan inside the drunken Takeo. Eventually he grew calmer. He looked down at Sachiko. His face was completely blank. There was no sign of feeling whatsoever.

Other neighbors had run over to see what was wrong. Hidaka, Someya, and Hashimoto all had their anxious faces at the door.

"It was like that almost every night," Iwaya said. "Takeo would drink and he would get violent. Shiro was terrified. He'd be shivering and shaking. He hated being left alone in his kennel. He howled so much that we let him sleep in the kitchen. I think it's because of Takeo that he's such a coward now. Is that right, Shiro?"

Shiro looked up at Iwaya cautiously. Iwaya stroked his head.

Shiro shivered again, as though something cold was running up his back.

"Poor Shiro!" said Iwaya as though talking to a little child. "You remembering it? Were you scared?"

"It's not Takeo that's bothering him; it's that!" Hashimoto said, gesturing toward Dad.

"What?" said Dad.

"There! In your hand…" said Hashimoto, pointing to the watering can Dad was holding.

He had let its nozzle drop, so that it was spraying water onto Shiro's back.

"Ah!" said Dad, straightening the can. "Sorry!"

"Takeo was so big!" said Iwaya. "Built like a bus. Once he lost his cool, you couldn't do a thing."

"Yeah. I tried to stop him once," said Someya. "Punched me in the mouth, that's how I got these."

He took out his false teeth and grinned, showing everyone the empty gums in the front of his mouth. It wasn't a pleasant sight. Shiro snorted and looked away.

"I feel sorry for Machiko," said Hashimoto. Like Hidaka, Hashimoto was normally a listener. He was quiet as charcoal. And just like charcoal changes color in different temperatures, the shade of his dark sun-burned face would show subtle variations, reflecting his state of mind. Now his face was showing spots of red, like glowing embers.

"People criticize Machiko for taking up with a man in town," he said, "but I can't see why she shouldn't have, after what Takeo did to her. All that violence. Crying every day. It was terrible for her. What had she done to deserve it? Takeo hit her every day long before she got another man. Of course, she'd want to leave him for someone else. We heard it all with our own ears—every single night! Takeo shouting and hitting her. Her screams. Him hitting Toshi. Yukihiro crying his heart out. Her screaming, 'Stop! Stop!' We all remember that. Machiko didn't do nothing wrong. It was all Takeo's doing. Everyone forgets. Everyone believes what Hatsue tells them, and they all say that Machiko's in the wrong. But it's Hatsue that's in the wrong!"

"That's true," sighed Iwaya, stroking Shiro. Shiro was sitting up and looking sadly into the distance.

Perhaps he was looking into the past.

"When Takeo was completely out of control, Machiko would come running over to our house with the children. He never came after them. I wonder how he felt, sitting there drinking on his own." Iwaya shook his head. "As for Machiko, she'd sit at our kitchen table sobbing."

Yukihiro looked anxiously up at his mother. She was shaking and sobbing, her hands pressed against her face. He sipped the soda that Sachiko had given him. The tension in his face melted as its sweet gentleness spread over his tongue, around his mouth, down his aching throat. Gradually he calmed down. The Iwayas' young son came and crouched next to him:

"Do you want to watch TV?" he said, looking into Yukihiro's face.

Yukihiro nodded and the boy took his hand. Yukihiro kept looking back at his mother as they headed into the living room, where there was a huge TV. Yukihiro's eyes were soon glued to the screen. He loved the big TV. He was happy. But he was sad. Because things were always the same when he watched this TV. His dad had changed into someone different from his dad, someone hitting his mom, hitting Toshi, hitting Mom, hitting Mom as she tried to protect Toshi, hands around Mom's neck, squeezing tight, squeezing tight, arms swollen, squeezing tight, squeezing tight, Toshi grabbing an arm but then sprawled in the corner of the room, hands squeezing Mom's neck, squeezing tight, squeezing tight, squeezing tight, Mom's eyes, looking at Yukihiro, tears falling from her open eyes, falling, falling, hands squeezing her neck, Toshi standing up, grabbing again the rough bulging arm, but then back in the corner, Mom's eyes looking at Yukihiro, tears falling, falling, falling, then Dad's voice, Mom's voice, Yukihiro's voice, all mixed up, and suddenly no sound at all, no sign of what had been in front of him, his mom, his dad, Toshi all mixed together, tangled up, something was spinning around and around, around and around, and then he realized he was at the Iwayas' house, and his dad who'd changed into someone different from his dad wasn't there, the hands around his mom's neck weren't there, and he was looking over at his mom sitting, her shoulders shaking, her hands over her face. Then he would forget for a while and be drawn once more into the world of the huge TV.

Toshi didn't go into the living room and watch TV. He stayed in the kitchen. Shiro was lying on an old bath towel on the floor and Toshi crouched in front of him, stroking his head and back. He said nothing. Sometimes he looked worriedly at his mom. She kept crying, her face in her hands. Sachiko was beside her, one hand resting gently on her back.

Iwaya sat across the table from them in silence. The TV blared from the living room. From time to time Yukihiro laughed. A minute ago he was crying, Toshi thought. Toshi stroked Shiro's back. The dog's eyes were closed in contentment. Its back was soft. It felt nice. Toshi stroked it while his mom kept crying. And as he stroked it, he was thinking. He was thinking about how to kill his dad. *I'll get him when I'm bigger*, he'd told his mom. *I'll show him!* His mom was pleased. *Yes*, she said, nodding. *When you're big, we'll punish him.* She smiled. She smiled happily. A secret promise between the two of them, sealed with a nod. Toshi kept stroking, kept thinking. Kept thinking about how to kill his dad. He wanted to grow quickly. Grow quickly and make him pay. He'd add everything up—all the times his mom had been hit, the times he'd been hit, every tear his mom had shed, every tear he had shed. Add them all up. Then he'd hit his dad exactly that number of times. Make him pay precisely that amount. Toshi kept stroking. He wanted to kill his dad. His throat grew sore. It was burning. His eyes and head were hot. They hurt. He was going to cry. He stroked Shiro's back. The tears were hot. They stung the broken flesh on his cheeks. It hurt. But still he stroked Shiro's back. As he stroked, he wiped his tears away with his other hand. He wanted to kill him. But how could he deal with such a huge man? Would it really be possible to grow bigger than his dad? But still, he wanted to grow. He wanted to grow quickly. He stroked Shiro's back. The tears stung his swollen cheeks. He wiped them away. His cheeks hurt when he touched them. He flinched and brought his hand away. Dejected, tears flowed again. His other hand kept stroking Shiro's back. He clenched his teeth and wiped the tears away. He stroked Shiro's back. He stroked.

"When he ain't drinking he's such a good man. None better."

Toshi's hand paused. He looked up.

"When he ain't drinking he's a good man. None better."

He couldn't believe his ears. All the pain faded for a moment. *What are you saying?* he thought. He couldn't understand it. What on earth was his mom saying? He'd stopped stroking Shiro's back and was looking up at his mom.

"Sachiko told her straight up," said Iwaya. "'You've put up with enough,' she said. 'Everyone knows that. Everybody understands. You've got to leave him, Machiko.' But Machiko just said, 'I won't.' If it'd been just once or twice, we wouldn't have said it. But as we all know, Takeo went berserk almost every night. It was terrible for Machiko and the boys. She came to our house all the time, crying. The boys'd go to bed and she'd still be crying. We let her cry all she wanted and then we'd tell her:

"'You've had enough. Nobody'll say nothing bad 'bout you. Why not leave him?'

"But she wouldn't agree to it. She cried all night long. Cried and cried. Not a wink of sleep, she must've been thinking about Takeo, herself, the children's future…everything. But she still wouldn't agree.

"'When he ain't drinking he's such a good man,' she kept saying. 'None better.'

"I couldn't believe it.

"'Machiko,' I said. 'You ever gone a day without Takeo drinking?'

"She didn't answer. She just repeated what she'd said before:

"'When he ain't drinking he's such a good man. None better. None kinder.'

"And then she cried.

"Sachiko rubbed her back. 'But Machiko,' she said.

"Machiko interrupted her and, looking straight into her eyes, said:

"'I love Takeo. I love him. I don't want to leave him.'

"It sounded like the truth. We both saw that. She meant it. She loved that idiot. So there was nothing we could do but just watch it happen.

"The next morning, she took the children by their hands and went back to the house. The little one cried. He didn't want to go back. He always cried a lot. But Toshi wasn't like that. He said nothing. He just went along with his mother. He was already taller than her, so it was more like him taking her hand than the other way around. He's quite a boy. Kept his mouth shut tight. Didn't say a word. Machiko always bowed when she left. 'Sorry to be a nuisance,' she'd say. 'Thank you!' Then she'd smile. 'I'm going to keep trying.'

"We knew she'd be back again that evening, but we didn't say anything."

Shiro shivered. Dad looked at the watering can, thinking he'd spilled more water. Silly man! The spout was facing upward, its nose high in the air like an insolent child. Water wouldn't drip from that.

No, it wasn't from the watering can. Shiro shivered again. Tears were dripping onto Shiro's nose. My tears. It was Mom's fault. She was looking down with her hands pressed over her eyes. I was crying because she was crying.

Dad gave us a worried look. His expression was so

dumb I burst out laughing. But the tears kept rolling. What a stupid face! Another tear fell on Shiro's nose. He licked it and looked up at me, puzzled.

"Violence passes from person to person," Iwaya said, tickling Shiro's neck. "And it builds up." Shiro's eyes narrowed happily. His tail thumped against the ground.

"Yeah," said Hidaka, "Takeo's father—Shei—was the same. He was a good fisherman and got along very well with Yoshi-nī's grandfather. But when he drank, he was even worse than Takeo. He didn't go wild like Takeo. He was quiet, but still very frightening."

"Yeah. Terrifying," said Hashimoto. "Like the eye of a storm. You think everything's settled down. You think it's over. But wait! Look! You're still right in the middle of it. You never know when it's going to end. You don't know what's going to happen. No way of guessing how strong the winds will be, what damage they'll cause. You keep wondering when it'll be over, but you just have to wait. Low dark clouds swirl around in your mind, and you can't relax for a moment. It's just terrifying. I used to stand in front of our altar at home and give thanks that I didn't have a father like that. 'Thank you! Thank you!'" Hashimoto rubbed his palms as though in prayer. "He was a big man too. Even bigger than Takeo. I was just a kid then, but it seemed like he was as big as a truck."

"It's because of violence. Because of hate," said Iwaya. "Violence makes a body bigger. The more a parent hits a child, the more hate builds up inside them. It swells up and makes their bodies thick and big. There ain't any hate in a child to start with. It's all in the

71

parent. But with every blow, a bit more of it gets into the child. The child takes in the parent's hate. It's made to. But the hate that makes the parent hit the child wasn't always in the parent either, of course. It came from the parent's parent. Through violence. Blow by blow."

"So, you mean anyone who's big was raised with a lot of beatings?" said Someya, astonished. He looked down at the false teeth in his hand, as though Iwaya's mention of violence had knocked them out of his mouth.

"That's right," said Iwaya. "Toshi's big because of all the beatings he's gotten from Takeo. And Takeo was hit a lot by his father, Shei, and that's why he grew big as well."

"So all big people have been hit by their parents?" Someya asked again earnestly.

"Yeah. Think about it. Did your father ever hit you?" asked Iwaya.

"What? Um. Let me think…" said Someya, folding his arms.

"Everyone always said what a good man he was," said Hashimoto nostalgically. "Yoshio the Buddha they called him."

"Well, no," said Someya. "I wasn't hit that often… But I once stripped my sister, tied her to a camphor tree, and looked between her legs. My dad hit me for doing that. Oh yeah, and another time, I'd been up at your hut in the hills, Hashimoto, and your dad gave me some charcoal, so I thought I'd put it in the shed at home. I opened the door and there was my dad, naked with my sister. I was astonished. My dad went red as an ogre and hit me very hard. I think that's all. Just twice," Someya concluded proudly. "He must have been a real saint."

"There we are then. That proves it. Look at you," said Iwaya, scrutinizing Someya.

He was only five feet one inch tall. He had to look up even when talking to my mom.

"You must have hit your sons a fair amount, then," Hashimoto said, staring at Iwaya.

Iwaya frowned. Both of his sons—truck drivers for Marugi Fisheries—were nearly six feet tall. The younger son was particularly big and strong. As a teenager he'd played for the prefectural rugby team and they'd reached the quarterfinals of the national tournament. The boy had smashed through the opposition's defense with the force of a Marugi Fisheries eight-ton truck and run fifty meters dragging three opponents behind him like bits of rag—or at least that was how Iwaya had, at least three times, described the scene to every single person in the village, with the only exceptions being Toshiko-bā, the housebound, and small children. He'd even told Mitsugu Azamui several times, though I doubt that Mitsugu, dragged around by alcohol, wearing away the ragged cloth of his existence, would recall having been told even once.

"Anyway, Shei-nī, Takeo's dad, was terrifying," Iwaya said, recovering his spirits. "He was odd, too. No question about that. It must have been miserable for Takeo when he was a child."

"Yeah, to be handcuffed by his dad in a pig shed," said Hidaka. "But why?"

"Yeah, why?" The Silica Four looked at each other and cocked their heads.

"Well, his dad was stranger than most. I suppose that's why."

Shei was trusted by the head of the Todaka fishing business, back before it became Marugi Fisheries. He was a particular favorite of the then-boss's father—Yoshi and Hatsue's grandfather.

Shei was the best pole-and-line fisherman in the village. He'd come back with the boat full of fish every time he went out. But it wasn't his contribution to the business that made the old man so fond of him. The old man had bad legs and couldn't get out of the house much; Shei used to carry him around. When Shei arrived at the house after fishing, the old man would slide along the floor from his room to the front door and look up at him fondly.

"You're big—that's why fish swim toward you!"

Normally the old man's eyes were lifeless. Like a fish's, they didn't focus on anything. But any time the old man saw Shei he sighed and his eyes sparkled like a child's.

Shei was really huge. The crippled old man was the only person in the village who'd ever seen the top of his head.

When he saw Shei, he would slap the floor fretfully, whining to get up on his shoulders. He was like a fish thrashing about on the quay. Senility was probably already setting in. And he deteriorated rapidly after the Midori Maru incident. Until then, though, his mind stayed on shore. It had been smoothed gradually by the waves of time but was not yet light enough to be washed away. But the Midori Maru took it, against the flow of the incoming waves, out to the open sea.

Shei, without a word, put his hands under the old man's armpits and hoisted the shrinking, desiccated body lightly onto his shoulders. The old man bellowed with delight. Bending carefully as they passed through the doorway, Shei walked out of the house and toward the bay.

As soon as the sea came into view the old man started shouting and slapping his hands against the top of Shei's head.

"Look, Kazuo! Sardines! Look! The fish trap! All them sardines!"

The old man was calling Shei by his own son's name. His daughter-in-law, Kiku, was following them. "I'm sorry," she said, looking up at Shei. Shei nodded but said nothing. The old man's fingers were fumbling restlessly through Shei's short-cropped hair, and drool was dripping from his mouth onto the big man's head, like fetid water from a gutter.

"Shei never says anything," said Kazuo to Kiku later, shaking his head. "Might as well talk to a rock. I sometimes wonder whether he can speak at all."

But Kazuo wasn't complaining. Even though he'd just had a new boat built, he'd been wondering who he was going to get to build the next one, now that the Kawano family was moving to Manchuria. But if they had Shei, they wouldn't need another boat anytime soon. He could do as much for them as any new boat.

Shei was certainly a quiet man, but words don't catch fish. A silent rock, he was beloved not just by the old man, but by "Ebesu-san" too, the sea-god. Just as the old man's senility enabled him, within a very narrow scope, to see particular details with great clarity, so Shei's rock-like physique was a blessing in the craft of a fisherman, for whom so much is under the arbitrary sway of Nature. Shei's size overwhelmed his small fishing boat, and from a distance he looked like a reef that had suddenly sprung up in the bay. Fish gathered in his shadow. He didn't have to go after them; they were there for the taking. They followed him in shoals, every fish rushing to find refuge in the shadow of Shei the rock. It was a large shadow, but there wasn't room for all of them, so the fish jostled at its edges, splashing above the surface of the water. Sometimes it sounded like laughter, sometimes a whisper, sometimes song. The sounds followed him across the water. That's why he doesn't have to talk, said the villagers, pointing out to sea. The shoals of fish following him in a silver spray—these were his laughter, his whisper, his song.

Shei was an itinerant fisherman—nobody knew where he came from. He just turned up in the village one day with his little son, Takeo, Toshi's father.

Like Azamui, Shiotsuki was a common name in the area. But Shei had no relatives there. Where was this Shiotsuki from? Everyone in the village was curious to know his background. Some tried asking him indirectly, but he said nothing. His size alone made him intimidating; his silence made him even more so. People gave up trying to find out. Shei was always silent, but the silence seemed all the more frightening when you'd asked a question that you thought perhaps you shouldn't have.

It was said that only three people in the village had ever heard Shei speak: Todaka Kazuo, Mitsu—Kazuo's cousin who worked at the village office—and Ninomiya, the policeman.

Kazuo was the first. Shei appeared in the village one morning before dawn. Holding his son's hand, he knocked on the Todakas' door. "Can you give me work?" he asked, bowing deeply. He'd brought a letter of introduction from a boat owner named Kanada in a village further along the coast. Kazuo had been in the same crew as Kanada when he was younger and they'd sailed all the way to the Korean peninsula, fishing for grunt. They'd been as close as brothers, and for Kazuo the scrap of paper in Shei's hand was enough. He cleared out a storehouse and prepared it so that the father and son could live there.

Kazuo's cousin Mitsu worked at the council's village office, so there were no problems getting the newcomers registered. It all got sorted out in advance. Mitsu liked Shei. Her husband had been physically weak and frequently ill. He'd died of tuberculosis the previous year. Looking after him had been exhausting, and she felt that if she ever married again it should be to someone like Shei, a picture of strength and health.

For certain documentation, it was necessary to write Shei's name. She knew his proper given name was "Seizo," but she didn't know the characters that were used to write it. She waited for him to come by, as he did every day, with his wheelbarrow full of fish. He was so big he made the barrow look like a toy.

"Shei-nī!" Mitsu called. "What characters do you use in your name?"

Shei stopped and looked down at her, expressionless as ever.

"If you don't want to say, that's okay," said Mitsu, as if she'd said something wrong. "I'll manage somehow." She didn't want to upset him.

"'Shio' like in 'shiotsuki' then 'tsuki' as in 'shiotsuki'; 'sei' like in 'seizo' then 'zo' as in 'seizo,'" he said, and walked off with his barrow. When she tried writing the name, she realized this hadn't been much of an answer.

The person who probably knew Shei's voice best was Officer Ninomiya. This wasn't because of any camaraderie between them as outsiders—Ninomiya was a villager, born and bred. And anyway, their interaction was far from what you might call conversation. Only Shei spoke, and the normally sociable policeman kept silent. He had no idea what to say.

Shei's power over the policeman unnerved the children, and they saw him in a very different light than the adults did. The adults tended to look on him with warmth, but the children, especially the boys, regarded him with absolute terror. They'd all seen it. Yoshi—the son of Todaka Kazuo—his friend Hachi, their gang of hangers-on, which included Hidaka, Iwaya, Hashimoto, and Someya, as well as Ken from the Bungo Strait guesthouse, and Tahara from the temple. They'd all seen little Takeo in handcuffs in the Todakas' barn. Real handcuffs. And they'd each—in their own particular way—suffered an intense and indelible shock.

Once young Kawano Itaru had left with his parents for Manchuria, the main target of ridicule for Yoshi and his little gang was the effeminate Tahara. Tahara tried as much as possible not to go anywhere near the Todaka house, not just to avoid Yoshi, but because the sight of Takeo in handcuffs in the barn was so frightening. When he thought of Takeo he felt a darkness inside his head—the black shadow of a giant, carrying handcuffs and stinking of fish. It made him cry. But unfortunately for him, he often had to go to the Todaka house with his father, the priest. It was the largest house in the village and funeral and other ceremonies were usually held there for family members of the fishermen the Todakas employed. The fishermen were always very grateful, because their houses were too small for family altars and all they had were mortuary tablets. Whenever such ceremonies were held, the young Tahara would have to go to the house to assist his father.

Every time he passed through the Todakas' gate he noticed the barn in the southeast corner of the garden. Inside was the empty pen of Midori, the pig which had been eaten to celebrate the completion of the new boat. Crouching quietly in the darkness of the pen was Takeo. He was large for his age, but still very young. In the next pen was a goat, flies buzzing all around it. You could smell it from the garden. Takeo was as still as a stone. He didn't move an inch, even when flies landed on his hands or feet. It was as though he were dead—except that his eyes were open, staring at the light from the garden. There were flies crawling all around his eyes, trying to slake their thirst. But his tears had dried long ago. His eyeballs glistened with moisture, but the greedy flies kept their filthy mouths and legs away. Perhaps they sensed that something inside those eyes was burning, seething. Tahara imagined his own image reflected in those eyes. The idea made him shiver. And there was something else gleaming in the darkness, besides Takeo's eyes. Amid the dry gray legs of pigeons and sparrows on the edge of the pen was a strange silver glint. A handcuff. And from there a chain, a line of light, fell toward the handcuff's twin, clamped tight around Takeo's tender wrist. How different from the rosary and charm that gently encircled Tahara's own wrist. The metal ring bit into Takeo's wrist, tearing at his flesh; and the blood oozing from his wrist bit back, gnawing at the metal. Every time Tahara saw that, he wished he'd done as his father said and spent more time learning the sutras. All that came to mind was a jumble of phrases from different sects. *Nan-man-dabu, nan-man-dabu, nan-myou-ho-renge-kyo, ma-ka-han-nya ha ra mi ta, kuwabara kuwabara.* He felt ashamed of himself. He should know more, coming from a temple family.

But why didn't the adults say anything? Why did Takeo have to be handcuffed in a pig shed? Tahara's father had no more to say on the subject than the other adults in the village:

"Takeo must have done something very bad. If you do anything bad, you'll get the same treatment. I'll borrow the policeman's handcuffs and put you in the Todakas' pig shed too."

Why had Officer Ninomiya lent Shei his handcuffs?

It wasn't that Ninomiya had particularly wanted to. They were government property, after all. And he was certainly someone who preferred to avoid trouble. That was why, at the time of the Midori Maru incident, he didn't say a word to the military police about the men.

There'd been something else at work when that giant came and asked for the handcuffs. Ninomiya simply couldn't say no. It wasn't that he was scared. Of course, he might have gotten hit if he'd refused, and the thought of that hulking chest and arms as thick as tunas certainly made him nervous in hindsight. But at the time, he had seemed to be under a kind of spell.

"Lend me your handcuffs!"

Almost before Shei finished speaking, Ninomiya had removed the handcuffs from his belt and handed them over. After that, whenever he saw Shei's great shadow crossing the road toward the police house, he'd simply placed the handcuffs on his desk and disappeared into the living quarters, entirely forgoing the special opportunity to talk to Shei.

"Amazing!" said Dad. "That'd be unthinkable these days. A policeman lending his handcuffs to a member of the public!"

"It was a long time ago," said Hashimoto. "When we were kids."

"We're getting old now, ain't we?" Iwaya said.

"That's true," said Someya, nodding. "Everything's different now. Everyone's changed."

They all looked at him.

"Your height ain't changed, Someya, you're still as short as you ever were!" Hashimoto said.

"That's the truth," said Hidaka.

"Mmhmm," mumbled Someya, uncertain what to say next. Then he grinned, his front teeth missing. A toothless grin. His teeth were grinning from his hand. A mouthless grin.

"What about the romance that started in the pig shed?" he said.

The other three shot glances at him as though he'd overstepped his bounds. Someya took no notice.

"Takeo took Midori's place," he laughed.

Hatsue liked her brother's classmate Kawano Itaru. She liked him far more than she did Abe Hachiro. Hachi was thin and swarthy. He had sharp features and deep-set eyes, as though a sculptor had gouged too deeply with his chisel. She never dreamed she would end up marrying him.

But her feelings for Itaru died away. It wasn't because she learned that they were related (Itaru's father was Hatsue's great uncle); Hatsue knew that a connection like that was no barrier to marriage. One of her brother's friends, Someya, had parents who were cousins, but he was still a much faster runner than her brother. So, being related like that didn't matter. That didn't stop her from liking Itaru.

It was Itaru's father who messed things up, when he made the mistake with the name she'd chosen for the boat. It was unbelievable! She was furious. And to think that it was Itaru's father who had built the boat with his own hands! Didn't he care about the things he made? Her anger didn't fade. It was the first time her father had given her, rather than her brother, the right to name a boat. And it was no ordinary boat. It was the reincarnation of Midori. Midori, who had been sacrificed to celebrate the boat's completion. And what made it even more terrible was that Hatsue had, without knowing it, eaten her, a part of her. Hatsue hated herself for that. She thought of Midori's eyes—clever, moist, green eyes—the reason she had chosen to name her Midori. Hatsue's own eyes grew moist as she remembered her. Midori had been naughty. Hatsue knew. She knew what her brother did, hiding in the barn. She knew why he was nasty to Midori.

Her brother's trousers were down. He was playing with his willy. Midori (her name was Momo then) grew excited. Mucus ran from her muddy, straw-covered snout. Saliva and bits of food spilled from her mouth. She shrieked. Her voice sounded just like a human's. She jumped up against the side of the pen, toward the regular movement of Yoshi's hand. Her body was shaking. She shrieked again. Then for some reason their mother came rushing in. She looked at Yoshi, shocked. Later, she told their father, who just laughed, long and hard. But Yoshi didn't find it funny. He blushed crimson as he watched his father laugh.

Yoshi was very annoyed about what had happened. That's why he put a firecracker in Momo's anus. He had no right to do a thing like that. He had no right over her at all. He took no responsibility for her. He never even fed her. It was always Hatsue who did that, taking out the family leftovers. Momo had a good appetite and powerful jaws that could crunch up any fish skeleton, even bream. But never having fed her, Yoshi had no idea her jaws were so strong.

The moment Yoshi put the firecracker into her anus, Momo twisted around and sank her teeth into his butt. It was so painful he thought it had been ripped in two. That's what he said afterward... A butt is always in two parts, though, so it seemed like a stupid thing to say.

Yoshi was so angry that he took Momo's name away. "From now on you haven't got a name. You're just a shitty nameless pig." Hatsue secretly gave her another name. Naming her made Hatsue feel like she was Midori's mother, and she grew fonder of her than ever. Hatsue loved to watch Midori munching her food, saliva dripping from her mouth. Midori would even try to eat the aluminum containers. It was so cute!

Yoshi couldn't possibly imagine how she felt, and so he didn't understand why she was so angry when Itaru's father made the mistake with the boat's name. To him it was funny, and he and his gang mocked Itaru about it at every opportunity. Itaru was the smartest boy in the class, which made teasing him all the more satisfying.

"Your dad can't write! Your dad can't write!" they jeered.

Itaru looked annoyed at first, but he said nothing back to them. After it happened a few times, he began to look sad, but that didn't bother Hatsue. She no longer cared about him at all.

Poor Midori! Hatsue pinched her stomach and then her arm. *Midori is part of this*, she thought. It made her heart ache. And Midori was now part of her heart. She was mourning Midori's death, with Midori right there within her.

Not long after, the Kawano family left for Manchuria. She couldn't remember exactly when. She wasn't sure whether Shiotsuki Takeo and his giant father arrived before or after the Kawanos went. But one day she noticed Takeo where Midori had been. He was handcuffed in her pen. He'd certainly been there before the Midori Maru left, because those men who disappeared on the Midori Maru had been in the barn at the same time as him. They were hiding there. She'd seen them. And that's not all. She'd seen her aunt Toshiko with one of them. They were in each other's arms. Hatsue had woken in the middle of the night and begun to worry that Takeo might still be in the barn. His father sometimes left him there handcuffed all night. She went out into the garden. It was pitch black—no moon, no stars. She could hear the waves. They sounded close enough to wet her feet. An owl hooted in the distance. *It's so quiet*, she thought. But just at that moment, she heard a voice. She was amazed. It was Midori's voice. It was the cry that Midori had made when Yoshi was playing with his willy. Is it her? Has she come back? Hatsue couldn't believe that. Perhaps it was her ghost. But she wanted to see her. The cry got louder and more intense as she approached the barn. Her heart was pounding. She went inside. She couldn't see anything. There was nothing there but Midori's cry. It seemed harsher and more strident than she remembered it. Her eyes gradually grew accustomed to the dark. *I'm going to see Midori*, she thought. But Midori wasn't there. Toshiko was there. She could see her face. Her mouth was open. Midori's cries were coming from her mouth. She was naked. The man on top of her was naked too. Toshiko and the man were together, clinging to each other, moving. Suddenly, the cry seemed frightening. Hatsue left the barn. She ran back to the house and got under her quilt, but in her head she could still hear Midori's cries. Midori wasn't there, though—not now. The cries were from that big writhing nakedness—naked Toshiko and the naked man, clinging together.

Very soon after that, the men left the bay on the Midori Maru. Takeo's father disappeared at the same time.

On that day too Takeo was handcuffed in the barn. Hatsue went inside and saw him there, where Midori had once been. But she wasn't thinking much about Midori this time.

What was in her mind now were Toshiko's cries. She crouched down in front of Takeo. The goat was in the next pen. It had watched in silence as Toshiko and the man lay moving in the back of the barn. Now it bleated. But its bleating didn't drown out the sound of Toshiko's cries. Hatsue put her arms tightly around Takeo's neck. His body stiffened for a moment in surprise. The handcuff clinked. But he didn't resist. She pulled his thighs between hers and moved as Toshiko and the man had moved. She rubbed her crotch against his thighs. She heard Toshiko's cries, but they were coming from her own mouth. They were *her* cries. She took Takeo's unshackled hand and pulled it against her growing breast. She rubbed against him. The handcuff clinked. Takeo squeezed her breast. His breath was uneven. The handcuff clinked. Hatsue felt Takeo grow hard against her thighs. She cried out, rubbing her crotch against his.

One way or another it would continue with Hatsue and Takeo. After his father left, Mitsu, Kazuo's cousin, would move in to the house to look after Takeo, but even then he and Hatsue would carry on in the corner of the barn. Officer Ninomiya's handcuffs, which had bound Takeo to the pen, were replaced by invisible cuffs binding the two of them together. Hatsue's mother, father, brother, and everybody in the village would eventually notice what was going on. But in spite of it her father would tell her to marry Abe Hachiro, Yoshi's classmate. And she would marry him. But she and Takeo wouldn't stop. And even if the people of the village thought it was happening, they wouldn't say anything, at least not in front of Hatsue, Hachiro, or Takeo. And in due course, Takeo would marry too. Hatsue thought nothing would change. And, in fact, they continued meeting, but she felt something wasn't the same. Bit by bit, things were falling apart. Takeo started drinking. Hatsue didn't like the woman Takeo married. She kept thinking about her. When she heard that Takeo hit his wife, she felt sorry for him. Takeo must be unhappy. Takeo had never hit Hatsue. It was the woman's fault. When she heard that the woman had left, she was glad. When she heard that the man she'd run off with had left her, she was gladder still. She felt a cruel delight. At the same time, she felt sorry for Takeo. The woman had shamed him. Hatsue would make things better for him. That's why she arranged it so that he could give up fishing and get a job at Abe Construction. And that's why she spent so much time making nice meals for his children.

Since they were his children, it felt as if they were her children too. If she'd had children of her own, then maybe her feelings toward Takeo might have changed. But she and Hachiro hadn't had any. Her feelings were the same as ever, and she didn't want them to change. So, when Takeo smashed the Marugi fish pens, Hatsue stubbornly resisted her brother's attempts to get him fired. Takeo hadn't been drunk, she said. He'd just been very unlucky. Anyone would have been upset if they dredged up a thing like that. Poor Takeo, she said. They'd probably stopped doing it. Perhaps it was a question of age. But…Takeo wasn't the same. He quit Abe Construction. Hatsue still made meals for his children: fried chicken; sardine burgers; deep-fried fish cakes. Perhaps the people of the village hadn't actually known about them after all, she thought. Hachiro might have, though. That couldn't be helped.

Then the Midori Maru came back. The same Midori Maru—no question about it. Things had begun between her and Takeo the day it disappeared. And now it was back. To signal the end? Hatsue didn't want to think that. No, it was bringing back the past, before they'd changed.

One night, Mr. Yoshida and I saw a black shadow fall into the sea from the Midori Maru.

It was a close, humid night. Since the afternoon, gray clouds had hung low in the sky. They looked like they might bring showers. I thought if they did, it would settle the air, cool it a little, like a sprinkler in the garden. But no rain came and the humidity intensified. Our bodies were saturated with heat and, instead of the clouds bursting, our skin erupted in a deluge of sweat.

We sat in Mr. Yoshida's car. In front of us, beyond the hills, I could see a large black cloud coming our way. It was swirling slowly, pressing down between the two headlands where the bay met the open sea. It was like gas released into a sealed space. It spread slowly at first, along the edges of the promontories. Then it moved quickly inward, covering the bay, until it had nowhere else to go. It kept low, licking the dark surface of the water, blending with the sea. It concealed every ridge and nuance of the mountains, smothered their graceful melody—now tight, now round, now sharp, now loose—so that the visual music which normally came through the darkness, from the deepest part of the night, could not be heard. All that sounded behind my eyes now was the black cloud and an ominous unease.

The black vapor throws the bay into convulsions. The surface begins to murmur and moan, the bay squirms. Fish are jumping, breaking the surface all over the bay. They're in pain. They cannot breathe. They fall, slapping back down against the water. The sound multiplies, grows louder. They're in pain. To get away from the pain they coil their bodies with all their strength and leap as high as they can, but then fall back, striking even more heavily against the hard, black water.

Eventually, the rain begins to fall. It subdues the bay, like a lid coming down on the swirling water. The black cloud pelts down its malice, forcing the fish to abandon their useless resistance. Wounded, robbed of breath, stifled, something in the bay dies. Blood flows and turns foul. I can smell the stench of rotting. We keep the windows closed.

The red tide was blood shed by the bay. It was blood sullied with evil and poison. I thought I could see a red stain spreading over the water. I thought I could. But even with headlights on, there was no way I would have been able to make out the color of the bay in the rain-drenched darkness.

The boat in the bay floated silently as the rain beat down. It was like a memorial to the victims of a disaster that had been wrought by humans, and yet was more terrible than humans could imagine. The plinth of that memorial was shaking. Shadows of death pressed around it. Shadows that couldn't get inside were pushed back. Shadows that didn't want to go inside tried to pull themselves away.

There was a splash. A shadow the size of a person dropped into the water, as though somebody had thrown a corpse overboard. The figure floated to the surface and moved slowly toward the bank. It was reminiscent of some giant tropical lizard, moving easily over a grass-green river—its rough head and back above the surface, as though crawling with its claws along a thick plank of water just a few centimeters below. But unlike a tropical lizard, it wasn't chasing prey, nor was it simply passing along a route that happened to be covered in water. It was escaping. From what, I don't know, but there was no question that it was escaping from something. When it reached the water's edge, the lizard resumed human form and crossed the beach. It walked along some rocks and disappeared up a slope, densely wooded with cedar trees.

The figure on the shore was not the only thing to escape.

We were all standing in front of the police house wondering what we were there to talk about. The thread of the Silica Four's conversation was evading us completely. A wind—cool, but heavy and humid—had started to blow in from the bay. It was pulling in the night, which lay out at sea, hiding beyond the eastern promontory. Shiro suddenly stood and walked out of the garden, wanting to go home. He reached the bridge over the creek and turned his head. But with no sign that his master, Iwaya, was following him, he plodded sadly back and resumed his position at Iwaya's feet. He walked off again several times, but back he always came, his tail sweeping wearily from side to side. The starting point of the discussion had been why the villagers didn't do anything about the boat floating in the bay. The Silica Four had said it was because nobody wanted to get involved in the argument between Hachi-nī and Yoshi-nī. But that was as far as the discussion had gotten. It just stayed there, with no sign of movement, like the boat itself. Listening to the Silica Four talk, I had no idea why Hachi-nī and Yoshi-nī didn't get along. I knew the red tides made the bay dirty, and that it had

been Yoshi-nī who decided that dredging was necessary to improve the convection current, and also that he
had decided to contract Hachi-nī 's Abe Construction
to carry the work out. I also had the impression, from
tying a few loose remarks together, that there was some
history between Hachi-nī's wife, Hatsue, and Toshi's
father, Takeo. But I still didn't understand why Yoshi-nī
and Hachi-nī had fallen out. I'd once seen an NHK
Education TV show in which a Western ethnologist
described the frustration people of his profession feel
when they can't get at the information they're looking
for. I was beginning to understand that frustration myself. Just when you think your informants are about to
tell you something, they go off on a tangent, recount-
ing anecdotes of no direct relevance. And not just that.
While they're talking other people come along and
join in. The flow of the conversation is constantly being
interrupted, or taken off in a completely different direction. The ethnologists begin to think that their sincere
attempts to discover truths about a society and culture
are being deliberately obstructed.

"But that's not the case," said the ethnologist,
whose research had focused on a tribal society somewhere on the Upper Nile. "For them, it's the normal
way of talking about the subject. We may think they're
digressing, but in their minds they aren't at all. And
what we find logical can be totally irrational to them.
So, we have to be careful with words like 'logic' and
'rationality.' And especially the word 'truth.' We can't
judge things by Western standards. It seems obvious,
but it took me a long time to realize that."

While I was watching the program, Dad and

Mitsugu Azamui were both deep in a drunken sleep, their mouths wide open. It wasn't yet ten o'clock.

To me the behavior of drunk people was totally irrational. I wondered if it might reveal some different "truth," but I couldn't for the life of me imagine what that "truth" might be.

Where was the Silica Four's conversation leading? Even my dumb dad was beginning to wonder. He turned to Someya:

"Sorry, Someya-san," he said, "but, well, in just a few words, what exactly were Yoshi-nī and Hachi-nī arguing about?"

"Don't be impatient, shenshei," came the response, not from Someya but from Hashimoto.

Here we go again, I thought.

"In a word," said Hidaka, who generally spoke less than the others, "the starting point was the fugitives."

"Fugitives?" said Dad, astonished. "Fugitives?"

"That's right," said Someya quickly to preempt the others. "Fugitives. They'd escaped and they came here."

"Do you mean Shei and Takeo?" said Dad, worried we might be about to listen to that story again.

"No, no," said Iwaya. "These men were miners."

"Sorry," said Dad apprehensively, "but when was this?"

"When we were kids," said Iwaya, puzzled by Dad's reaction.

Dad hung his head despondently.

Oh, no! I thought. *Where are we off to now?* When on earth would we get to the reason for the argument?

It was like trying to use one of those robotic claws

at an arcade. You always bring it down too close or too far away, failing to get the cuddly toy. The more irritated you get, the farther from the target the arm comes down. You have to keep calm. I thought of the ethnologist's face. He was a quiet old man, but when he smiled his eyes sparkled mischievously. I pictured his bald, egg-shaped head.

"It was a shock, wasn't it Someya?" said Hashimoto.

"It was astonishing. We were coming down the hill from your charcoal place."

The two boys were coming down the path that ran through the hills.

"Excuse me!" said a voice behind them.

The boys turned in surprise and saw three young men. They looked dirty, as though they had traveled a long way. They wore work clothes covered in soot and mud, frayed and torn. They were all well-built and about the same height. Their heads were shaved. They actually looked as if they could be from the village. But the boys were sure they weren't local. It wasn't because of their hollow cheeks or the exhaustion in their eyes. That wasn't unusual at all. What was unusual, though, was the way they spoke:

"Is there anywhere we can obtain water? We have come a long distance and we are thirsty. We are also extremely tired."

The boys stared at each other, rooted to the spot.

The man sounded as if he were reading from a school textbook. For the two boys, especially for Someya, being told to read a textbook aloud was the worst thing that could happen at school. He was extremely jealous of Hashimoto, who, living in the hills and helping his father with his timber business, hardly ever came to school. Only the day before Someya had been asked to read. He'd stumbled through the passage very slowly and even then, missed two lines. The teacher had been furious. "But nobody talks like that," Someya had wanted to retort. But here were three people in front of him who spoke exactly like that.

The men were Korean workers who'd escaped from a coal mine in Nagasaki. They told Todaka Kazuo very willingly that they hadn't come to Japan of their own accord—they'd been forced to. They didn't know why. All they wanted was to go back to Korea.

The boys had taken them to the Todakas' house, where the men of the village gathered to hear what they had to say. Kazuo was listening carefully. He glanced at Shei, who was sitting next to him. The great rock—motionless and silent as always. Golden rays of afternoon sun gathered on the rock and dozed. Perhaps the weakening light found reassurance in Shei's large, firm body. The women were watching the proceedings from the room next door. They looked worried. What was going to happen?

The problem was the authorities would never let the three men get away. They'd never turn a blind eye. The military police—the kempei—would be after them already. If they were caught, they'd face appalling punishment. The kempei were terrifying. So much so that mothers no longer threatened their naughty children with a visit from a ghost ship. Instead they told them to expect a knock on the door from the kempei.

"Let 'em go!" A loud voice cried from the hallway. "Let 'em go!"

Everyone turned. It was Kazuo's old father. He was supposed to be taking a nap in his room, but he'd come crawling down the corridor. Drool hung from his mouth, but he kept shouting:

"Let 'em go! Let 'em go! Don't do the same thing again! We can't!"

To the three fugitives this seemed like senile babble, and to Someya and Hashimoto as well, who were sitting behind the village men. But Kazuo and the rest of the villagers knew immediately what he was saying, and why he had forced his broken body to crawl out from his futon.

"Okay," said Kazuo. "They can hide till things calm down."

Of course, it would have been dangerous if they'd hidden in one of the houses, and they didn't want to be a nuisance, so it was agreed that they'd stay in the barn. Kazuo thought it was the perfect place. If the kempei discovered them, the villagers could just say they'd had no idea there was anybody there.

"Yoshikazu!" Kazuo shouted for his son. "Go and get Officer Ninomiya!"

When they heard the word "officer" the three fugitives turned pale. Hadn't the man just this moment said they'd be protected? Perhaps they'd misunderstood. Everybody was speaking a dialect very different from the type of Japanese they'd been forced to learn. The Koreans couldn't understand everything the villagers said. And perhaps the villagers hadn't really understood what the Koreans said.

Everyone had been smiling so they'd thought what they'd said had been accepted and that the villagers felt goodwill toward them. How stupid they'd been to smile back! They'd thought they were going to be protected, but perhaps the decision had been exactly the opposite. Rather than being hidden in the barn, were they simply going to be kept there until the police came? Isn't that huge, rock-like man going to say anything to help? At least *he* must understand what we're saying. Is he just going to abandon us?

Nobody knew what Shei thought, but Todaka Kazuo didn't have the slightest intention of abandoning the Koreans. He'd been surprised by his father. The old man still had sense. He still knew what he was talking about. People who forget the past repeat it. We have to remember. We have to atone. And now the opportunity had come.

"That was the first time we heard anything terrible had happened in the village," said Someya.

And now *I* was hearing it for the first time. But Someya said anyone from the village over a certain age would be familiar with the story. They'd all have heard it talked about once or twice in their homes.

It happened a long time ago. Before the old man, Kazuo's father, was born, people said. A boat from somewhere far away took shelter in the bay. The people on the boat looked just like the people of the village— they were of similar height and had similar faces—but they spoke a very different language. Their clothes were beautiful and their boat was splendid—very different than the village's simple fishing boats. The villagers were fascinated. They thought there must be treasures hidden on the boat, wonderful things they'd never seen or heard of.

But after a while, the villagers grew irritated by the outsiders' incomprehensible language. They couldn't stand it. Then one day something seemed to collapse, and before anybody knew quite what was happening, they'd killed all of the outsiders, torn off their clothes, and seized their boat. The first person both to cut a throat and to go down into the hold was from the Azamui family.

But there was nothing there. At least, nothing of any value. Or, rather, there was just one small wooden box, but Azamui slipped it between the folds of his clothes without telling anyone. The villagers wanted to hide the evidence of what had happened, so they sank the boat in the middle of the bay with all the bodies inside. Some noticed what Azamui had done, but they said nothing. They had all done appalling things. It terrified them to think about it. For there to be at least one person even worse than they were seemed to lighten their burden a little. Everyone knew what was in the box: *Look! His family's suddenly so well-off! Better look now, though, before it's too late. The dead men's curse will catch up with him sooner or later. Or, if he's too quick for it, it'll get his children or his grandchildren. It'll swallow them up.* The Azamui family grew. Though other families were hesitant to forge marriage connections with the Azamuis, the number of Azamui children grew quickly anyway and the different branches of the family multiplied. *But, look! See? They've had a blind child. They've had a dumb child. The old man was so quick on his feet, but now his grandson has had a child who can hardly walk.* The curse had finally caught up with the Azamuis. That's what the villagers thought. But they'd actually been wrong all along. There had been nothing in the box. It was completely empty. He'd thrown it away. He hadn't told anyone. He couldn't—nobody would have believed him. He didn't sleep at night for regret about and fear of what he'd done. He couldn't relax for a moment. That's why he was so active, why he worked so hard—he was trying to forget. And because he worked so hard, he grew rich. As for the curse that people gossiped about...if it came it came. It didn't bother him. He was cursed already. A curse from which he would never be free. A curse of memories he would never forget.

Of course, nobody believed these days that the Azamui family was cursed. The Silica Four all agreed on that.

"If your family grows and you have a lot of relatives, then you're bound to have more poor ones," said Hidaka. "The proportion of poor relatives in any family is about the same. You can't just look at the absolute number in isolation."

That seemed to make sense.

"Yeah, and it's the same if people marry in their own family," said Iwaya. "If they're too close, the number of unlucky children goes up."

"But it's hard to believe that Mitsugu ain't cursed," said Hashimoto.

The rest of them immediately burst out laughing. Dad joined in.

"How 'bout Toshiko-bā then?" Someya said. "It's hard to believe she ain't cursed too!"

His roar of laughter this time was met only with awkward glances. The atmosphere had suddenly soured.

"Well, I think I'd better go inside," Mom said, sensing the tension. "I've got to get ready for a trip tomorrow."

"Oh?" said Someya, looking at her gratefully for changing the subject. "You're going on that women's association trip, are you? My wife's going too. Have a nice time!"

"Thank you!" Mom said. She bowed to everyone, then bent down where Shiro was lying. "Bye bye!" she said softly. Then, straightening up, she went indoors.

"Such a nice lady!" said Someya when she'd gone. The rest of the Silica Four nodded in full agreement on that.

Dad didn't look too unhappy at this, but perhaps to hide embarrassment, he laughed and said, "Well, maybe on the surface..."

I decided I'd report that to Mom.

"Speaking of trips," said Hashimoto, "when are Yoshi-nī and Hachi-nī due back from Malaysia?"

"It ain't Malaysia," said Someya, "the Philippines— an assembly trip to find out about bringing back the remains of soldiers killed in the war."

"What?" said Hidaka. "Where'd you hear a story like that? It ain't got nothing to do with war dead. I heard directly from someone who works with the assembly. There's an idea to build a resort somewhere down here in the south of the prefecture and a bunch of assemblymen from local districts have gone to Guam on a fact-finding mission."

"That's rough!" said Someya. "Guam's really hot."

"Rough? Don't be stupid. They say, 'fact-finding mission,' but there's no fact-finding involved. They've gone there for a vacation! Nothing but fun!"

"What?" Someya said. "Using our taxes? Mr. Kawano will be furious when he finds out!"

Someya seemed to have forgotten that Mr. Kawano always described the Silica Four as "tax bandits."

Dad was pretending not to hear what they were saying.

"Anyway, with Yoshi-nī and Hachi-nī away," Iwaya said, "nobody can do nothing about the bay. It practically belongs to Yoshi-nī, so if anybody did anything they'd end up in a fight with him—just like Hachi-nī."

While his son went to get Officer Ninomiya, Kazuo asked his wife, Kiku, to take the three Koreans to the barn. They'd been worried about the word "officer," but they saw no sign of deception in Kazuo's eyes, so they decided to trust him. They followed Kiku to go and hide.

Soon afterward, Yoshi returned with Ninomiya. The crowd in the garden made way for the policeman. He looked worried. Kazuo came out of the house and sat down, cross-legged, on the veranda. He looked Ninomiya in the eye.

"I want you to do something," he said.

"I know," replied Ninomiya. "I've been contacted by HQ. They say some Koreans are in the area. Yoshi told me that's what you wanted to talk about."

Kazuo glared at his son, who looked down in embarrassment.

"Then it won't take long to explain," said Kazuo, turning back to Ninomiya. "What did your HQ tell you to do?"

"The same as always: 'Take necessary action as soon as possible.' In other words, they want me to find them and arrest them."

"As I expect you know, I have no intention of handing them over," Kazuo said firmly, "and my father feels the same."

Kazuo turned and looked into the room behind him. Shei was sitting on the floor and the old man had climbed onto his shoulders. When his son looked into his eyes, the old man started hitting Shei's head in excitement. Jolting violently from side to side, drool spattering from his mouth onto Shei's head, he shouted:

"Don't do it again! We can't! Let 'em go!"

As always, Shei's face showed no expression. His massive arms were clamped over the old man's thighs, preventing him from falling.

"That's what I mean," said Kazuo, turning back to Ninomiya. "You're related to the Azamuis, so you'll understand."

"I don't mind, Kazuo-nī," said Ninomiya. "But the kempei are on their way. They'll find out sooner or later."

Bored children in the crowd started whispering excitedly at the mention of the kempei.

"I'll act dumb and stall for as long as I can," said Ninomiya.

If the kempei were after them, the lay of the land meant it would be almost impossible for the fugitives to escape on foot. The village was situated on a small peninsula on the Pacific coast. From there a series of narrow capes reached out eastward, like feelers fumbling for the morning sun. The village was near the tip of one of these capes. At the base of the cape was a town with a railway station. And along it were smaller promontories, like suckers on an octopus's arm. These promontories formed little bays, and the village was on the bay at the eastern end. To escape on foot, one would first have to reach the base of the cape. But the kempei would obviously be coming from that direction, where the railway station was.

Kazuo knew very well that it was just a matter of time before the kempei arrived and he wanted to do what he could to help the men escape. He wanted to respect his father's wishes. His father had told him the story of the foreign boat many times when he was growing up. Kazuo didn't really believe it. His father hadn't witnessed the events himself—he'd simply been told about them by his own father. And probably Kazuo's grandfather had been told by his. In his grandfather's day, the Azamuis had still been prosperous. It was they, rather than the Todakas, who'd controlled the village's fishing then. The Todakas were just fishing folk who worked for the Azamuis. Kazuo didn't know exactly how his grandfather had taken over, but *something* had happened between his grandfather and the Azamuis. That was for sure.

Sometimes he wondered if the old story was true after all. He wondered if what people called the curse on the Azamuis had been a product of people's envy—jealousy at the Azamuis' prosperity. Perhaps that was what his father meant when he shouted, "Don't do it again!"

Letting the three Korean laborers escape wouldn't mean complete liberation from the past. Kazuo didn't think it was that simple. But they'd been brought across the sea against their will. They'd have been leading very ordinary lives in Korea—in small villages not much different from this one. Kazuo could imagine it—he'd often fished off the Korean coast when he was young, and he'd been to a lot of villages there. Cheated or threatened, they'd been taken from their villages and brought what, under the circumstances, must have seemed a very long way across the ocean. If that had happened to Kazuo, he'd want to escape, he'd want to go home. So he wanted to help them. Would that atone for the Todakas' past, for the village's past? Could it? There's no coming back from death. There was nothing he could do about that. But he was determined to help these men escape. We can't do it again. That to him was the only unshakable fact. His father knew it, even in his senility. He no longer walked, he'd abandoned self-awareness, he'd returned to the very threshold of evolution, he was in reach of a place where life and death were inseparably entwined, but even then he'd shouted:

"We can't do it again!"

Kiku took the three fugitives to the barn. They were astonished by what they saw there. The sun was going down and it was very dark inside, but they could make out a boy, crouching by the nearest pen. The men looked at each other. They would never have imagined finding a child there. His right hand was handcuffed to the pen. When they saw the handcuff, they remembered the day they were taken. They felt a jumble of powerful emotions: anger, fear, and shame at their fear. But this child—why did this child, large for his age, but still clearly very young—why did he have to be handcuffed?

The fugitives had been nervous already, but Kiku realized that the sight of the child made them tenser still.

"Shei-nī!" she shouted from the doorway.

Within moments, the great rock was blocking her field of vision. Shei was walking toward her, the old man on his shoulders. He crouched low as he came through the doorway so that the old man wouldn't hit his head. Without a glance at the fugitives, he knelt on one knee in front of his son and took hold of the handcuff that was biting into the wood of the pen. A glob of drool dropped from the old man's mouth onto the handcuff, like oil intended to improve the function of the lock. Shei rubbed it into the handcuff, then pulled.

There was a loud clunk and the handcuff opened. Kiku and the three men watched in amazement. Shei opened the ring around his son's right wrist in just the same way. It was so easy—as if they had never been locked. But a cuff locks automatically as soon as the ring comes together. Had this giant simply pulled the handcuffs apart with brute force? If he had, you'd expect a grating sound. But there was nothing like that and the metal hadn't bent. Shei took Takeo's hand and pulled him up. Takeo picked up the handcuffs from the floor. With the old man still on his shoulders, Shei left the shed, leading his son by the hand. When Takeo saw Ninomiya standing in the garden talking to Kazuo, he let go of his father's hand and ran toward him.

"Here!" he said, holding the handcuffs out to the policeman.

The three fugitives couldn't believe their eyes. Kiku too was astonished. She wondered if the old man might be able to explain Shei and Takeo's extraordinary behavior. But she quickly abandoned the idea of asking him. The only answer she was likely to get was a froth of saliva.

Kiku's sister Toshiko had come to help at the Todakas' house that day. Kiku asked her to take some rice and soup to the three men hiding in the barn. Toshiko was amazed to see how greedily they ate, but then they'd had almost nothing to eat or drink for five days before reaching the village.

"We are very hungry," said the youngest of the men, who'd introduced himself as Go.

"The food is delicious. Thank you!"

The next day Toshiko took them breakfast. Her niece, Hatsue, was with her. Shortly after he'd finished eating, Go stood and went outside. For some reason Hatsue hurriedly stood up too and followed him. Behind the barn was a pit for feces and urine. Go waited beside the pit for Hatsue to leave.

In the end he couldn't wait any longer and said:

"Excuse me. I have to use the toilet."

"I wanna see," Hatsue said, her eyes gleaming.

They'd been gone for some time, so Toshiko came

out to look for them. Astonished to see Hatsue near the pit, she grabbed her hand and pulled her away.

"What do you think you're doing? Come here!"

"I wanna see his poo," she said.

The blood drained from Go's face. He looked heartbroken. Toshiko knew immediately what was wrong. Hatsue must have heard a well-known song that ridiculed Koreans. Toshiko felt terrible.

"I'm sorry! I'm sorry," Toshiko apologized, bowing again and again. "You silly girl!" she said, smacking Hatsue's head.

Hatsue started to bawl.

Go crouched down in front of her.

"Do not cry! Please do not cry," he said. "Everybody's poop is the same."

He smiled and stroked her hair.

Hatsue looked at him.

"The same? It ain't cold?"

"Everybody's is the same," said Go gently.

Toshiko imagined his pain, seeing such terrible prejudice infecting the innocence of a child. It had left him speechless for a moment, but now he was smiling, brushing it aside. She sensed the pain was still there, though, deep inside him.

As Toshiko watched Go smile and stroke Hatsue's hair, she felt affection for him. It rose from the ground in front of her, from that mire of shit and piss and food waste where maggots flickered like small white flames, it rose like a gentle wave. A pleasant warmth spread up through her calves. Her tension eased. That was the start.

"What set it all off," said Someya, his teeth now securely back in place, his hand no longer hovering in front of his mouth. "What set it all off was when Takeo's crane dredged up the corpse from the bottom of the bay."

"A corpse!" exclaimed Dad. It looked as if we were finally getting to the heart of the matter.

I thought of the joy felt by ethnologists who were at last getting the information they were after, their informants finally beginning to respond in the right way. But should the ethnologists be happy? Might that happiness be simply because they were hearing the informants say things they wanted them to say, things that were already in the ethnologists' minds?

"Well, I didn't see it myself," said Someya. "It was Mitsugu, wasn't it?" he continued, looking for confirmation from the other three and Shiro.

"Yeah. Mitsugu said he found a body. Made a huge fuss about it," said Iwaya. "I never saw it either, though."

"Nor me," said Hashimoto. "But Mitsugu went on and on about it."

"He wouldn't stop, and then Takeo went and caused that accident," said Hidaka. The others all nodded. Shiro thumped the ground twice with his tail.

"In the end, the only person who believed Mitsugu was Hatsue," Iwaya said. "She wanted to protect Takeo, so she said it only happened because Takeo saw a body. It wasn't his fault at all, she said."

"Sorry, I don't understand," said Dad. "What exactly are you talking about?"

It happened a short while after Abe Construction had started dredging the bay. Takeo was operating a crane, pulling mud from the seabed. The mud was loaded onto trucks and dumped on the beach at the end of the promontory. Then, as now, Mitsugu Azamui was often at the beach. He'd sit with a bottle, looking at the sea, gradually growing sleepy. Then he'd stretch out on the sand and fall asleep. Then the sea would come in and the wind would blow, and he'd wake up wet and cold. Moving to a dry spot on the beach, he'd start drinking again to warm up. Then he'd fall asleep again. But the trucks were coming and going the whole time, so the smooth shell of his sleep was constantly tainted by noise. He kept trying to disinfect it with alcohol, but just when he thought all impurities had been removed, the noise would return as yet another truck dispersed its load of mud onto the beach, staining once more the surface of his sleep.

Mitsugu stood up angrily. He looked up at the mound of mud that the trucks had tipped onto the beach. It looked and stank like excrement. Columns of dung flies, constantly re-forming, pierced the mound, like children poking it with sticks. A child thrusts his stick in, pulls it out, inspects the end, grimaces at the smell, holds his breath, recovers, thrusts the stick in again, and stirs it around. A loose piece flies up and the child jumps to avoid it, then looks back at what remains. There's now a hole, and through it something can be seen.

That was how Mitsugu found the corpse in the mound. The crane's iron arm had gouged into the silent seabed, pulling up everything there, everything that had disposed of life and was gradually turning into mud. Exposed to the air and sunlight, the tumult of decomposition intensified.

And in that uproar the corpse shouted loudest, like a speaker trying to get the attention of an audience. The flies were the spray of the speaker's voice, his spittle, his sweat. Their countless wings astir, they crammed the appalling smell into Mitsugu. He felt sick. He pressed his bottle to his mouth and the little liquid that remained flowed down his throat. His throat burned. He coughed. He vomited.

What came out were just foul-smelling gastric juices tasting of alcohol. He sank down onto the sand and looked up again at the mound of mud.

Mitsugu told everyone in the village about the body. He seemed obsessed. He went to where the trucks were parked and demanded that someone take it away—it was polluting the beach. Most of the workers ignored him. They thought the drunken Mitsugu Azamui was just seeing things.

Hidaka was a manager at Abe Construction at the time.

"Mitsugu was making such a fuss that I went over with Takeo at lunchtime to check whether there was anything there," he said.

When they arrived at the beach, Mitsugu was standing on top of the mound, foraging in the mud. A hot wind was blowing off the bay. The billowing waves showed glimpses of white where they caught the sunlight.

"You keep piling all this up, and now the body's

disappeared!" he shouted, covered head to foot in mud.

He'd brought various things out of the mud. Scattered around the two men's feet were glass bottles, pieces of wood, a rusty kettle and pan, a chipped cup, and some empty cans.

"Tell us where it is, Mitsugu," said Hidaka.

Mitsugu Azamui ignored the question. He kept on pulling things out of the mire of sticky mud and throwing them down toward the two men. They moved back to avoid the shower of trash.

Hidaka was getting angry.

"Mitsugu! Stop messing around! Where's this body of yours, you drunk?"

Mitsugu Azamui kept on foraging. His expression was intense, so perhaps he hadn't heard. Hidaka's words weren't what he was looking for, any more than were the jumble of items he'd pulled out of the mud. Like the trash, the words were things to be carelessly cast aside. He threw down yet another item.

Takeo picked it up and stared.

"What's the matter?" asked Hidaka.

"Look at this," said Takeo.

He was holding two rusty rings linked by a rusty chain. He held them up. Through the rings, he could see the black bay heaving in the wind. They were handcuffs. He looked stunned. A deep sigh shook his great frame, like a blast of air from a bellows. His sunburned face grew redder still, like iron in a blacksmith's furnace.

"If you fools keep piling on more mud, the body'll never be found!" Mitsugu yelled into the wind blowing from the bay.

"I knew what Takeo was thinking," said Hidaka. "It was tough on him. By then he wasn't drinking and getting violent like he had before."

"Yeah, he changed a bit after Machiko ran out on him…but only a bit," Iwaya said, stroking Shiro sadly. "I mean, when he drinks now, he still hits his boys."

"True, people never change much," said Someya. "I haven't grown at all for decades. I'm still as small as ever." He grinned, his teeth all in perfect position.

Unfortunately for Someya, nobody else smiled. Shiro didn't even look at him. He just stood up and walked quickly away.

"It was that afternoon that the accident happened," said Hidaka, following Shiro with his eyes.

They went back to work, leaving Mitsugu Azamui shouting and foraging madly in the mud on top of the mound.

The plan was to start dredging a new area that afternoon. The location presented some challenges, so Hidaka was feeling tense. It was on the far side of the bay and moving the crane meant passing through an area packed with Marugi Fisheries' yellowtail pens. There was a clear route, used by the boats that fed the fish. It was easy to get fishing vessels through, but the channel would only be just wide enough to allow the passage of a large marine crane. Hidaka recommended to the boss, Hachi-nī, that they take a detour just to avoid anything going wrong. A detour would take quite a long time, especially because it was windy and rough. So, with this suggestion, dredging wouldn't start until the following day. Hachi-nī clearly didn't like that idea. He told Hidaka to be up and running at the new location that afternoon. They were already behind and Hachi-nī didn't like to extend working schedules. So that was that. Hidaka couldn't go against the boss's wishes.

Hidaka piloted the tug that pulled the crane across the bay. As they approached the pens, the sea began to heave under their floating walkways, like the chest of a panting animal. Seabirds on the walkways saw them coming, flapped their wings, and flew up into the air with raucous cries. The birds were soon joined by others who'd been resting on more distant rafts or flying high above. They'd noticed the excitement or seen the boat's approach and flocked together, wheeling and screeching, thinking the tug was bringing feed for the yellowtail. They were waiting for it to be scattered, like seeds on smooth, black, damp ground. The streamlined, leaf-shaped young fish, full of life, would then burst up from the black water, as though the strength of the sun had coaxed a shoot from each small round pellet of feed. Then, hungry for the young fish, the birds would descend, letting out the air held in their wings.

But it wasn't the birds that broke the membrane of the water that day, plunging into the sea.

There was a deafening roar, as if something had exploded underwater. The tugboat lurched heavily to one side as spray pelted down on the deck. Hidaka gripped the wheel tight and managed to restore balance. He turned his head to see what had happened.

It was terrible. For a moment the blood drained from his cheeks, and then he was awash with sweat.

It burst out of him like a wave crashing on a levee. It mixed with the seawater that drenched his face, stinging his eyes.

The arm of the crane was sticking out to one side of the barge on which it was being carried. The dredging bucket that should have been visible at the end of the arm had disappeared. It was in the sea. That huge, voracious iron mouth was no longer satisfied, it seemed, with its repulsive forced diet of mud soup. Now it was devouring yellowtail—not just fry, but fully grown, fat, white-stomached adults. With a roar that wrenched at the very roots of existence, it smashed through the line of fish pens. Writhing in a seizure, the crane flung its arm back and forth, as though at the will of the savage and voracious dredging bucket.

Hidaka rubbed his eyes and looked in dread toward the crane's glass control cabin. Was Takeo all right? What had happened to him? Hidaka looked carefully. Takeo seemed fine. In fact, he was strangely calm...or that's how it appeared to Hidaka. Takeo's face was composed, placid—a complete contrast to the scene of devastation in front of him. His eyes didn't seem to be reacting to the orgy of destruction on the bay. He knew what was happening. Only too well, perhaps. He was moving the controls with his usual steady efficiency.

The bay, its core ripped out and crushed by the jaws of the dredging bucket, seethed and spumed with silver blood.

"It was astonishing," said Someya. "Everyone was so quick."

The villagers realized right away there was something wrong at the Marugi fish farm. They saw the Abe Construction crane moving oddly over the expanse of pens, and they heard the terrible sound of destruction. It was distant, muffled by the wind and by the rush of waves breaking on the shore. But there was no doubt it was caused by the swing of the crane's arm. Wherever the arm touched the sea, cascades of silver rose from the surface as if by magic. It was the yellowtails—jumping and dancing. They were like an oppressed people who had been liberated. Everyone wanted to join this ring of joy. They wanted to celebrate together. Driven by this feeling the villagers all rushed to the quay or the shore and launched their boats. Everyone was welcome aboard. But of course, there was one person who had no place in the ring: Yoshi-nī. What had happened meant a huge financial loss for Marugi Fisheries. He watched sourly as the flotilla raced over the bay, white wakes crossing here and there as the boats all converged on the spot of seething silver offshore. Deep inside, he must have been boiling with rage.

"We could take as many as we wanted," said Someya nostalgically. "Once they'd escaped they weren't anyone's property."

"It was our lucky day. Everyone was happy," said Hashimoto.

"I gave four or five to Officer Yamamoto," Someya told Dad.

"Ah!" said Dad, glancing at me. "I remember Yamamoto sending us some yellowtail in a chilled pack. He mentioned someone had given it to him. It must have been then."

"Yeah!" Someya said proudly. "They must have been the ones I sent."

For the yellowtail, though, freedom came at a high price. A lot of them were caught by the villagers, and a lot were killed by the dredging bucket itself. The next day dead fish kept washing up on shore, especially on the beach at the end of the promontory. Their corpses lay rotting in the sun, their lidless eyes gazing for eternity on the instant of their death. The combined stench of the dredged mud and the fishes' decomposition made the beach unbearable, and for a while almost nobody went near it. The only person who could stand it was Mitsugu Azamui, protected by the robes of his own alcoholic miasma. The King of Hades, he pressed his scepter-bottle to his lips, while, from the summit of his mud-mound, he surveyed his retainers, lined up on the threshold between sea and land.

"Mitsugu-san," said Dad when Mitsugu Azamui kept suggesting that, rather than a deer, it had been Toshiko-bā that he hit with his new car, "I did not hit Toshiko-bā. It was a deer. No question about it. I hit a deer and I killed it. We got rid of it ourselves. We were in the tunnel and I was driving too fast. Someya and the rest of them were talking about how good the acceleration was, so I thought I'd put my foot down even more. It was a new car and the tunnel was straight, so I wanted to give it a try. And then, right in front of me, was a deer. And that was that. Bam! Smashed right into it.

"I got out right away and looked at the front of the car. It was a real mess—covered in bits of bloody flesh and fur. It was all over the place. I was scared and I couldn't look at the deer. It must have died on impact, I suppose. It flew right to the edge of the road. Hidaka said we'd better get rid of it, so he and Hashimoto picked it up, crossed the road, and threw it down the hill on the other side. Hidaka took the front legs and Hashimoto the back legs—or 'leg' rather, since there only was one still attached. The other had been ripped off in the accident. It was Someya who picked that up. He took it over and chucked it down the slope as far as he could. Before throwing the body, Hidaka and Hashimoto swung it back and forth a few times. And when they were doing that, I saw the deer's eye. It seemed to stare right at me. It looked very sad and I realized I'd done something awful. I felt terrible about it."

Just then there was a cough. A persistent, hacking cough. Dad and Mitsugu Azamui were surprised and looked around to see where it was coming from. I knew it was an asthma attack. I left the kitchen and went through the living room on my way to Keiji's room. When I opened the door to the hallway there he was, hunched, crouching on the floor. I rushed to his room, found the inhaler in his backpack, and brought it right back. He used the inhaler while I rubbed his back. He'd been in the corridor listening in on the men's conversation. He must have heard Dad talking about deer. Being so fond of animals, it would have caught his attention. But what Dad said to Mitsugu was completely different than what he'd told us. It wasn't something he should have heard.

"Why did Toshi's father do a thing like that?" I said. "Why?"

Up until then I'd been listening in silence, but I couldn't stand it anymore.

From what the Silica Four had said it still wasn't clear why relations between Yoshi-nī and Hachi-nī had deteriorated either. I couldn't see cause and effect anywhere. "We mustn't expect a magic mailbox." That's what the ethnologist I'd seen on TV had said. "When encountering a different culture or even just another person, we tend to look for a mailbox that contains only letters that we want to read. But of course, they don't have such a mailbox, any more than we do. There's no such thing."

But before the Silica Four started talking about something else entirely, I wanted to be given a reason. That might not have been the right attitude if I'd been an ethnologist, but I wasn't. *I'm sorry*, I said silently to my bald-headed professor.

"Yes, why?" Dad said as well.

"Why?" said Iwaya. "You want to know why Takeo did it?"

The Silica Four looked at each other.

"He must have wanted to break up with Hatsue," Someya said with a smirk.

The other three glared at him. So did Shiro, who had come back to lie at Iwaya's feet.

"Perhaps he was remembering his father," said Hidaka.

"That was quite a way to die," Someya said sadly.

"So, his father's dead? Is there a direct link between that and the crane accident?"

"You can't say for certain it's direct," said Iwaya, "but we think there is a connection."

The kempei finally arrived in the village. The officer in charge was short and plump, and he was flanked by two taller men—a round-shouldered one with a toothbrush mustache on his right, and a younger one on his left. Standing together they resembled the character for "river": 川. They seemed certain the fugitives were in the village, and on arrival at the police office the plump one said simply:

"Where?"

"What do you mean, sir?" Ninomiya said.

"Where?" he shouted.

"What..."

Before Ninomiya had finished speaking, the officer on the right gestured toward him with his chin: the younger one on the left leaned down toward Ninomiya and belched.

"Where are the Koreans?" he grunted. "You understand Japanese? Or are you from Korea too?"

Ninomiya hesitated.

The officer in charge gestured to his right.

A boy was walking by, head down.

"Hey! Young man!" the subordinate called out in a wheedling voice.

The boy was Tahara, from the temple. He stopped

and looked up, shaking—men he'd never seen before, and with them was Officer Ninomiya. He looked nervously at Ninomiya's hips, as if searching for something. No, no handcuffs. Tahara was on his way back to the temple from the Todakas' house. What he'd just seen in their barn hadn't been his imagination. Shiotsuki Takeo, handcuffed in the pen where Hatsue's pig, Midori, had once been. Tahara couldn't remember his sutras. He didn't even try. "If you don't try," his father—the priest—had threatened, "I'll do what Shiotsuki Shei does—I'll borrow Officer Ninomiya's handcuffs and put you in the pig shed!" Did Officer Ninomiya really lend out his handcuffs to anyone who asked?

"Hey!" The kempei officer stepped toward him, releasing him from nightmarish thoughts of handcuffs.

"Seen anyone you don't know?"

Tahara pointed.

"Over there?" the officer said.

Tahara seemed to be pointing somewhere beyond where the officers and Ninomiya were standing.

"Is that right, boy? Over there?" the officer said, his mustache bristling.

Tahara felt uncomfortable. The officer's breath smelled of tobacco. Tahara thought he'd better point more accurately.

"Here, there, and there," he said, pointing carefully at each of the entirely unknown kempei officers in turn.

Meanwhile, Todaka Kazuo was hurrying the fugitives toward the Midori Maru. Hashimoto, the lumber dealer, had reported seeing some unfamiliar men crossing the hill toward the village. The Midori Maru wouldn't be missed. It had just been built, and it wasn't yet in use. Their two older boats had brought the Todakas prosperity and meant a lot to them. They didn't feel that same kind of bond with the Midori Maru. The new boat hadn't developed any character yet. It was colorless and transparent. It was odorless— it hadn't absorbed the smell of fish and the sea. Kazuo prayed that that's how the boat would remain to anyone looking for the men—they wouldn't see it, they wouldn't smell it, and then it could escape.

The fugitives, standing on the deck of the Midori Maru, bowed repeatedly to Kazuo, Kiku, and the other villagers who were gathered on the quay. Kazuo noticed there was something between his wife's sister, Toshiko, and Go. Separated by ground and water, unable to touch hands, they were touching each other with their eyes. Shei and the old man weren't there. They were on the beach, beyond the quay. The old man was on Shei's shoulders, hitting his head and shrieking, with saliva flying from his mouth:

"Look! The trap, Kazuo! The trap! It's full of fish! It's overflowing! Hurry!"

"I'm over here, Dad," Kazuo muttered with a smile. Then immediately he was back to the task at hand.

"Quick! Before the kempei get here," he said to the Koreans. "Off you go! Take care!"

The villagers untied the mooring ropes, the wind filled the sail, and the Midori Maru began to move slowly away from the quay.

The next moment, there was a deafening noise. The kempei officers were in sight and the small one in

the middle seemed taller than before—he was holding a pistol over his head from which emerged a flash
of flame. The three of them were running down the
beach toward the quay.

"Stop! Stop!" they shouted as they ran past Shei
and the old man and then on into the little crowd at
the quayside. But the boat, blown by a gentle wind off
the hills, was moving slowly toward the mouth of the
bay.

"Get a boat!" screamed the commanding officer,
seizing Kazuo by the folds of his kimono. "Follow
them!"

His two subordinates, imitating their superior,
each grabbed a villager:

"Give us a boat!" they shouted.

"What do you mean?" said Kazuo, unperturbed.
"They've just gone fishing."

The officer struck him across the head with the
butt of his pistol.

Some women in the crowd screamed, "No!"

Their cries were drowned out by a louder voice.

"Go on! It's going to be a huge catch! Hurry!"

It was the old man. He was lying on his stomach
on the beach, scraping up and scattering sand.

"Look, sir," said the younger kempei officer to his
superior.

Shei was rowing a small boat toward them from
the beach, heaving at the oars with all his extraordinary strength. In no time at all the bow smacked
against the quay's stone wall. The three kempei officers climbed aboard. Shei hit the quay with his
oar, turned the boat toward the bay, and set off after

the Midori Maru. It had all happened in a moment. The villagers stood in amazement. Kazuo watched, speechless, as the boat moved rapidly away. What was Shei thinking? He rowed on and on. The Midori Maru had quickened, its wake showing white on the ultramarine of the bay, but Shei was pulling ever closer. Yet something was very different than usual about Shei's boat. Everybody noticed it. There was no laughter, no whisper, no song—the fishes' song, Shei's song. The sun was shining brightly on the bay, on the Midori Maru, on the villagers. Shei's huge rock-like shadow stood out in sharp silhouette. But where were the silver bubbles that always crammed into the shadow's darkness? Where were the fish? Shei was silent, as he always was on land. Something began to move toward his boat. A triangular dorsal fin broke above the water. Then another. And another. Sharks. Sharks were following Shei. The kempei officers didn't notice—their eyes were fixed on the Midori Maru.

"Faster! Faster!" shouted the commanding officer, waving his pistol.

"Hurry! Hurry!" came the voice from the beach, like an echo.

At that moment, Shei cried out. Everyone heard it. His voice thundered. The silent sea was ripped open and filled with harsh, brain-splitting noise. It was as if a vast mass of the earth's anger, held deep in the sea, had exploded. The shadow of the huge rock named Shei seethed, spitting up spume. Fish jumped and scattered like sparks, consuming the surface of the water with silver flames. The sharks plunged into the flames like a random spray of bullets; the sea roared.

Beyond the flames stood Shei. He had pulled the three officers together. He took the commander's handcuffs and secured the man's wrist to his own. The cuff was small for Shei and it dug into his flesh. It looked as though it might break at any moment. He took the mustached officer's handcuffs and secured him to the youngest officer. He then put his arms around them both and pulled them against his huge chest. There was the sound of pistol shots, but they couldn't stop Shei. Without a moment's hesitation, he jumped into the field of flames.

For an instant the villagers saw the flames turn red. Then they died away and the bay was quiet, as though nothing had happened at all. The Midori Maru was no longer in view. The waves undulated gently in a soothing breeze. It was as if the two boats had never existed. But the old man was still lying on his stomach on the beach, his hands thrashing around in front of him. No words came from his mouth, no cry—just thick globs of sticky drool.

"So that's what happened," said Iwaya.

"You talk like you actually saw Shei-nī die, but you didn't," said Hashimoto.

"You didn't neither," said Iwaya, dismissively.

"None of us did," said Hidaka.

"We heard about it from our parents," said Someya. "We'd been told to go up to the Todakas' house and stay there. We were in the barn with Takeo. But we certainly never saw Shei in the village again."

"It was a shame for Takeo," said Iwaya, stroking Shiro's back sadly, "not to be there when his father died."

"That's true," said the others, nodding. Shiro nodded too.

I stayed with Keiji for a while to make sure he was okay after his asthma attack. His chest was still pounding. It was like a stormy sea threatening to swallow him up. But the inhaler gradually took effect and his cough calmed.

"Dad…killed…the deer," he said. It was a struggle for him to speak. He made a hissing sound like escaping gas, as though each word were punctured. He was sitting on his bed with his back hunched and tears in his eyes. It could have been because he was sad, or just because of the coughing. Keiji's eyes and the deer's eyes seemed one and the same.

"You'd better go to bed," I said.

He climbed under his quilt.

"Stay here till I go to sleep," he said weakly.

"Okay," I said, "I'll turn out the lights."

When I got back to the living room, Mr. Kawano was there. I looked at the clock. It was just before 11 p.m.—the time he usually came to pick up Mitsugu Azamui. A little earlier, Mitsugu had been awake and talking with Dad, but now he was asleep. His face looked like a death mask, its expression fixed for eternity.

"Hello, Mr. Kawano," I said. He was on the sofa beside Mitsugu, talking to Dad. He looked up.

"Hello, Miki-chan…" he said. "Well, I should be taking Mitsugu home."

He stood up and started to pull Mitsugu to his feet. Dad, who was very drunk, tried to get up to help, but collapsed back into his chair. Mr. Kawano put his left arm around Mitsugu's shoulders and dragged him toward the front door. I noticed Mr. Kawano's fingers on Mitsugu's shoulder, the ones he couldn't bend. He was well over seventy. I wasn't so much surprised at his strength, as by the fact that Mitsugu could be so easily moved around by an old man. I held the door so that it was easy for them both to get through.

"Good night, Miki-chan," said Mr. Kawano.

"Mr. Kawano," I said, "when Dad was talking about the deer he killed, Mitsugu Azamui said he wondered if it was really Toshiko-bā. He told Dad she'd said she wanted to die. Dad was drunk and didn't take it seriously. But is Toshiko-bā okay? And is there really a corpse, like Mitsugu Azamui says? Yesterday we were talking with Hidaka-san and the others, and none of them had seen it. Where is it?"

Mitsugu was looking like a corpse himself, his head drooping against Mr. Kawano's neck. Mr. Kawano stared into my eyes. He looked sad. There were deep lines between his eyebrows and around his eyes, as if the night were carved into his face.

"Miki-chan, you've heard about lots of different things very quickly. You must be tired. I'll tell you about it some other time. You look sleepy—you should go to bed."

With that he left, dragging Mitsugu Azamui along with him.

"Good night!" he called back through the darkness. There were no streetlights. "We better not fall in the ditch!" he laughed.

I don't suppose Mr. Kawano ever forgets to think about others, I thought.

It wasn't long before I had the chance to hear more from Mr. Kawano. I was sitting one night with Mr. Yoshida in his car looking at the sea. Before we'd put the seat-backs down we saw Mitsugu Azamui on the beach. When we put them back up again, we weren't sure if he was still there.

The bay was sound asleep, rocked by the light of the moon. Its quiet breath was the lapping of waves, enticing watchers into the shallows of sleep. Out on the water, as always, was the Midori Maru. We were used to it floating there now. It hadn't moved at all. It must have been at anchor, but the question of who had dropped the anchor didn't bother us much anymore. The boat was a minor note in the melody of the moonlit bay and surrounding hills. Only someone with a keen eye would have noticed it at all.

There was a movement in front of the car.

"Must be Mitsugu Azamui," said Mr. Yoshida. "Let's give him a surprise."

He switched on the lights. Caught in the sudden glare, a figure turned toward the car.

"Oh, it's Mr. Kawano!" Mr. Yoshida exclaimed. "He must have come to take Mitsugu home."

Mr. Kawano came over to us, his face contorted in the bright beam. He tapped on the driver-side window. Mr. Yoshida opened it.

"What are you doing here?" Mr. Kawano said. He sounded very sad.

Mr. Yoshida looked uncomfortable. He said nothing.

"A teacher...in a car like this!" Mr. Kawano said, tapping the roof of the GTR with the unbending fingers of his left hand. "What do you think you're doing, bringing one of your students out here?" He glanced at me. "What's she going to learn from you in a car in the middle of the night? I'd have thought you'd have better things to teach her. You're social studies, aren't you?"

"Do you and Mitsugu-san want a lift to the village?" said Mr. Yoshida, ignoring Mr. Kawano's remarks.

"You're supposed to be a teacher, but you give them no proper education," said Mr. Kawano angrily. "That's why the boys don't stop shooting bottle rockets at Toshiko-bā's house."

"No point me tellin' them," said Mr. Yoshida, slipping angrily into dialect. "I did it all the time when I was their age. I can't start lecturin' them now! Anyway, that Toshiko-bā—one look at her and any kid would wanna chuck fireworks at her."

That's going too far, I thought, *even if he's angry*. I was worried Mr. Kawano might get really furious. But there was no sign of that. He just sighed...a heavy sigh, laden with sorrow.

"None of you know anything about Toshiko-bā. That's the problem. The older people in the village must know, but they keep their mouths shut. You know nothing because we've told you nothing. I go around telling kids not to fire rockets, but that's all I do. I've never said anything more. So, what gives me the right to lecture you? What've I ever told you about Toshiko-bā?" He was looking away toward the bay as he spoke. He sounded wretched.

"Miki-chan, you asked me about Toshiko-bā the other day. And you asked if the corpse that Mitsugu talks about is really there. I don't know whether that corpse is real or not, but the Toshiko-bā in the village today is very different than the Toshiko the villagers used to know. That Toshiko's no longer alive. She died in Manchuria—killed by her own countrymen. The Toshiko-bā in the village today is like that Toshiko's corpse. Toshiko-bā came back from Manchuria a corpse.

Young Kawano Itaru had seen his cousin Toshiko all the time when they lived in the little village, but Manchuria is a huge place and once they were there, they didn't often meet. At first, Toshiko lived with the Kawanos, but Itaru was staying with other relatives in the capital, Hsinking, where he was studying for the Kenkoku University entrance exams. He only came home once a month, if that.

After he passed the exams, he moved to a university dormitory, and by that time Toshiko was living in the colonel's house, where she and his father both worked. So Itaru and Toshiko saw even less of each other than before. But whenever he went home, his father talked about her. He was worried about her relationship with his Korean and Chinese assistants. Itaru's father may have shouted at his assistants, but he didn't despise them. So when Toshiko shared food with them, he certainly didn't object. In fact, when

Itaru told him that at the university dining hall everybody ate the same mixture of white rice and sorghum, he snorted.

"Why wouldn't they?" he said.

He was not well-educated himself, but to him it went without saying that an education system should treat everyone equally. Manchuria's national slogan was *Five Races under One Union.*

"What the hell does that mean if the Japanese are given better food than other races?" he said.

When the colonel was away and he ate lunch with Toshiko in the kitchen, he'd tell her to cook plenty of white rice. He never said as much, but he seemed to be expecting her to give some to his young assistants so that they'd get a good meal. "Eat up!" he'd shout with a smile. "You can't do a good job unless you eat properly!"

All this was okay in the colonel's large garden, where nobody was watching. But outside, there were dangers. Toshiko seemed to get along particularly well with one of the assistants, a well-built young Korean. He'd seen them walking along the road together. It worried him. If she was too friendly with Koreans or Chinese, she'd attract the attention of the kempei, who were constantly on edge about dissident activity.

That's exactly what happened to Itaru in Hsinking. He was suspected of having close connections with Chinese communist and Korean nationalist student groups. The kempei arrested him, along with a number of Chinese students. Before being tortured— *interrogated* was the word the kempei used—he was told that his father had been arrested in Harbin.

Toshiko and the young Korean had gone into hiding and the kempei thought Itaru's father must know where they were. The kempei suspected the young Korean of being Go Kim Ga, a powerful figure in an underground anti-imperialist organization. He had also recently been identified as one of the perpetrators of the murder of some of their officers in Japan.

Itaru's interrogators told him to give the names of students who were in "The Assembly." They punched him. Then they hit him with batons. He didn't know what "The Assembly" was. He told them so. They beat him more. They smashed some of his teeth. It wouldn't have been surprising if his father had helped Go escape. He may not have been educated, but he was a principled man and hated injustice.

And for him there was nothing more unjust than the kempei. In the streets of Harbin, kempei officers would beat Chinese, Koreans, or Mongolians over the most trivial matters, behavior for which a Japanese wouldn't even have been reprimanded. Itaru's father had always frowned in disgust when he saw that kind of thing happen. During his beating, Itaru thought of his father with pride. At the same time, he suspected that he was no longer alive.

Itaru was certainly interested in communist thought. He sympathized entirely with the Korean and Chinese students who longed for independence from Japanese imperial rule. He spent much of his time with them. But he had never been a member of what the kempei officers called "The Assembly." They kept on hitting him. Every time he said he didn't know, the beatings got more severe. Perhaps "The Assembly" was just an invention, an excuse to hit people, kick them, break them, destroy them. Who was hitting him? Who was kicking him? His eyes were filled with blood and tears, and he could not distinguish between the different figures. They were vague shadows flitting through his mind, along with sparks and flashes and the sound of tearing flesh and breaking bones. Then, through his weakening consciousness, he suddenly felt a searing pain. The nails of his left hand were being wrenched out, one by one. He no longer knew what his mouth, full of blood and vomit, was saying. The pain intensified. He struggled to see his left hand through the narrow gaps between his swollen eyelids. His third and fourth fingers, nails gone, drenched in blood, were jutting out at a strange angle from the rest of his hand. He couldn't understand anything anymore. But the kempei wouldn't let him lose consciousness so easily. He heard a voice. Someone seemed to be shouting. The shout and a terrible pain were burning his ear:

"Still can't hear, fucker? How about now?"

He pressed his suddenly unfamiliar left hand to his ear. But there was no ear. Just hot, sticky blood clinging heavily to his strange hand. He fainted.

He didn't remember much after that. He didn't know how long he was detained. He woke and from time to time through the iron bars of his cell he saw bodies being dragged past. One of them was that of a Chinese student he had been arrested with. His friend looked so different now that, at first, he didn't realize who it was. He closed his eyes. The dry sound of a body being dragged along the ground stayed with him. It was stuck fast to the left side of his head, where his ear used to be. Sounds came closer and then went further away. Itaru no longer wanted to open his eyes.

The next thing he knew he was in a crowd of refugees fleeing down the Korean Peninsula from the Soviet army, which had invaded from the north. He had no idea what was happening. Everyone was starving. Some had abandoned their elderly and children. Women, scared of being raped, had shaved their heads and put on men's clothes. He didn't know why he was walking. Was he walking in a nightmare or was he having a nightmare as he walked? He didn't know and didn't care. When he finally reached the port and saw the dark swaying ocean, he lost consciousness again.

He woke up in a corner of a large shipping warehouse. Almost everyone around him was frail from injury or sickness. The building was being used as a makeshift hospital. He could hear groans in all directions. It was very hot. He looked through a large open door and saw the summer sun reflected off the sea. The glare hurt his eyes. He knew then that this was reality.

Pus was oozing from where his ear had been. Flies swarmed around the wound. But he was better off than most. Many of them had maggots in their wounds. The sweltering warehouse was filled with groans and sobbing.

It was there that Itaru met Toshiko again. But she was no longer the Toshiko he had known. She was in no condition to look after it, but she had a child with her, about a year old. A young woman who had fled with Toshiko to the port was looking after both of them. Toshiko noticed Itaru.

"Itaru-chan?" she said in a rasping voice.

He didn't believe what he was hearing. It was like a distant memory lingering in the place his ear should have been. At first, he hadn't realized there was a person there at all. She was lying on rush matting on the floor, wrapped in bandages, filthy with blood and pus. She didn't have the strength to wave away the flies that settled on her wounds. The young woman with her, holding the little boy in one arm, brushed the flies away and picked out the maggots. Toshiko had lost her hair. Her face was covered in cruel swellings and burns. Itaru didn't recognize her.

"Itaru-chan?" she repeated.

"Toshiko-san?" said Itaru.

The other woman looked at him, then down at the bandaged figure and nodded.

Then, as if his presence had given her energy, Toshiko began to talk, though pain made her break off frequently.

When Go Kim Ga learned the kempei were after him, he took Toshiko to hide with friends in a village near Harbin. Toshiko was already pregnant and while in the village she gave birth to a boy. She named him Mitsugu.

Go was often away from the village, on underground activities. One day, the wife of Go's friend came to see Toshiko. Her face was pale. Go and her husband had been arrested by the kempei. She'd been brought the news by another man in their organization, who had managed to slip through the kempei's net. He had told her that she and Toshiko must escape. Then he disappeared. Toshiko was utterly desolate.

When she had seen Go again in the colonel's garden her heart had stood still. It must have been the same for him. After he escaped from the bay on the Midori Maru, she never imagined that she might see him again. But there he was. Her uncle was introducing him to his assistants as their new coworker.

Go was delighted when Mitsugu was born. Toshiko didn't tell him about what had happened with the colonel. She couldn't say it, and she didn't think she had to. Life was hard trying to evade the kempei, but as long as she was with Go, Toshiko was happy. But now he'd been caught and there was no hope for him. Toshiko cried. But crying wasn't going to help. No matter what happened to her, she had to look after Mitsugu. She couldn't go back to Harbin. She'd heard through contacts that her Uncle Kawano had also been arrested by the kempei. She was plagued with guilt by the news. She thought it was her fault.

Where should she go? She decided to rely on Kimie, a slightly younger woman she'd been at school with in the village back in Japan, but who was now in Manchuria. Carrying the bare essentials, she took Mitsugu and headed for Botanko, where Kimie lived. She walked along a wide roadway through fields of sorghum. The sorghum was like fur on the back of the earth; the road was a deep wound cut across it. Her steps were heavy. Her legs were pulled down by weariness, by the earth's silent endurance of pain. Unable to bear it, the earth began to groan. Toshiko stopped and stared at the ground at her feet. The groan grew louder. She lifted her face and looked down the road. In the distance, she saw trucks—Kwantung Army trucks—roaring toward her. She hid in the sorghum. Three trucks drove past. The backs of the trucks were covered with awnings, so she couldn't see what was in them. She felt a strange dread. She noticed that peculiar smell again. The trucks were followed by a black limousine. She could see right inside. In the back seat was the colonel. There was no doubt it was him. She saw his neatly trimmed mustache, his eyes—the same emotionless eyes that had stared out at the pitch-black garden. The vehicles shrank into the distance, sending up clouds of dust behind them as they continued toward their destination. Toshiko knew. She knew what was on the trucks. Her husband, Go, was there. She knew. He wouldn't come back. The smell welled up from the depths of her memory, the smell of that putrefying, putrefied poison. It choked her. She couldn't breathe. She clung to Mitsugu and cried. She cried as though her voice would splinter and break.

At Kimie's place in Botanko she began to show strange symptoms. She developed a fever. It lasted several days. Then her throat began to swell—her neck grew as thick as a log. Mitsugu was frightened when he saw it and wouldn't stop crying. The pressure in her throat made it difficult for her to breathe. Lying in unimaginable agony, she was convinced that Go was suffering in just the same way. The stench of the poison rose from her body. Just as the Japanese army's control of Manchuria was beginning to collapse, Toshiko's body began to collapse too.

Her hair fell out. Her fingernails hardened and grew black. They dropped from her fingers like magnolia seeds from a tree. Agony flowed like lava through her body. It burst through the surface, engulfing everything in its path, burning her skin and leaving behind festering black scars and smoldering pain; then it moved on with ever greater fury. Soviet armored divisions were sweeping into Botanko. Kimie took Toshiko and Mitsugu and fled. Time and time again on their journey, Toshiko begged Kimie to go on without her. But with the help of other refugees, Kimie managed to get her to the port. As they waited for an evacuation ship, Toshiko realized she could no longer move. In tears she asked Kimie to leave her and take Mitsugu. "I don't care what happens to me," she said. Kimie couldn't even tell that the reddish liquid coming from Toshiko's eyes was tears. It could have been blood or pus. And of course, little Mitsugu didn't know. Yet for Toshiko it didn't matter in the slightest what it was—all that mattered was Mitsugu's life.

Only Itaru and Kimie were allowed onto the evacuation ship. Because she was so ill, the army doctor said he couldn't let Toshiko board. The ship was simply there to evacuate people to Japan—it had no medical facilities, and Toshiko might die during the voyage. Itaru retorted that the doctor simply didn't want the crew to have to bother with Toshiko as a passenger. "I said no," said the doctor. If Itaru kept arguing, he might be refused passage himself. But at that moment he didn't care, even if it meant being killed by the Soviet army that was sweeping south behind them. But Toshiko pressed her deformed hands together and begged them both:

"Take Mitsugu back to the village! Help him!"

Itaru resolved to go. The army doctor promised to

take care of Toshiko. It was no guarantee, of course, but it seemed better than nothing. Itaru took Mitsugu in his arms and went aboard with Kimie. Kimie was sobbing, her head leaning on Itaru's shoulder. Mitsugu, not knowing what was happening, looked up at each of their faces in turn.

"And this is the same Mitsugu," said Mr. Kawano, looking at Mitsugu Azamui, fast asleep in the back of Mr. Yoshida's GTR. He was lying face up with his mouth open. "After we arrived back in the village, Kimie and I got together and looked after him. We decided we should do our best for him until Toshiko came back."

"But Toshiko-bā did come back," said Mr. Yoshida. "Why did you keep looking after him?"

The GTR had just passed the Marugi Fisheries plant, where a light was on in the office. Someone keeping watch on the place, I thought.

"Well," said Mr. Kawano, looking down pensively. "When she came back, nobody else seemed to realize who she was. But Kimie and I knew immediately. We were delighted—we never thought she'd come back alive. We took Mitsugu to her right away. He must have been three at the time. When we arrived, before we'd even said hello, Mitsugu saw Toshiko and burst into tears.

"'Mommy! Mommy!' he cried, clinging to Kimie's neck. 'I'm scared!'

"He refused to look at Toshiko again.

"'Toshiko-san, here's Mitsugu,' we said.

"'I don't know that child,' she said. 'I don't have a child.'

"I looked into Toshiko's sad eyes and I understood. Even then, I was going to say something, but Kimie looked into my eyes and said:

"'Don't, Daddy.'

"'Don't, Daddy,' she said. It still hurts to think how Toshiko must have felt.

"At that moment, Kimie and I swore to ourselves that we'd raise him. And we went back home. We never had another child, so this is our only one. Kimie did all she could for him. Mitsugu knew that Toshiko was his real mother—we told him. A parent is a parent after all. So he knew it, and then the silly boy...the silly boy...let us all down..."

Mr. Kawano ran his fingers through Mitsugu Azamui's hair, stroking it lovingly. Then he hung his head and quietly began to sob.

Mr. Yoshida pressed his foot down on the accelerator. The GTR Turbo snarled softly, like an animal protecting her young, sheltering Mr. Kawano's sobs from the deepening night.

That night I hardly slept. I got up very early the next morning and went to Toshi's house, among the Silicon Palaces. Toshi was already up. He was in front of the Iwayas' house next door, petting Shiro.

"Morning!" I said.

"Morning, Miki-chan! Why are you up so early?"

"I want to ask a favor," I said.

We were on a fishing boat and Toshi stood at the helm. With a practiced hand he turned on the engine. Its roar seemed to tug at the hem of the purple-tinged sky. Other boats were already on their way out to sea, leaving white traces on the surface of the bay, like chalk lines on a blackboard.

What had they written there? We didn't know. The traces were illegible, distorted by waves from our boat. And whatever it was our boat had written soon became illegible too. But we carried on drawing our white line across the bay, cutting through the waves. We were heading for the Midori Maru.

As we drew closer, there was a subtle change in the air. The fresh, new-born smell of the morning sea began to resemble that of the sea at dusk, when yellowtail feed and hot sun have been kneaded together all day. Then, as we got even closer, it was more like the smell of a bucket of seawater with rotten shellfish in the bottom. The stench grew and grew. It was hard to bear. Toshi stopped the engine and allowed the boat to float toward the Midori Maru. Grimacing, he tied a rope to a ring at the stern. I kept my fingers tight over my nose.

The heavily built Toshi clambered with difficulty onto the Midori Maru.

"Ugh! It stinks," he said, covering his nose and mouth.

He pulled me up after him. The whole boat was like a huge piece of rotting carrion. My head spun. A swarm of huge flies hung in the air overhead like the smell of death itself. Another swarm rose from a fish tank on the foredeck. The tank was crammed with yellowtail. Its water had been transformed into a glutinous, cloudy liquid—a chemical reaction with the death that oozed from the rotting fish.

"It's horrible!" I murmured with my mouth and nose covered.

With the buzzing of all those flies, I could hardly hear my own voice.

Toshi looked down some steps into the boat's hold.

"I'm going to have a look," he said, bending over to descend the steps.

"Agh!" he shouted.

"What's the matter? Are you okay?" I shouted down the steps.

"I slipped," he said.

When he eventually came back up, his face was drenched with sweat. He was carrying a magazine.

"What was there?" I asked. "What's that?"

"This?… Take a look…" he said, embarrassed.

He passed it to me. It was a foreign porno magazine. Naked women displaying their genitals. It made me even more nauseous.

"Come on, Miki-chan. Let's go!" said Toshi. He sounded worried.

"It this all there was?" I asked, recovering slightly.

"There's not much down there," he said, wiping the sweat from his face. "Blankets, empty cans… Somebody's obviously been here. Must have left, I suppose."

"I'm going to have a look," I said.

I slipped past him and went down the steps.

"Don't!" I heard him say behind me. "There's nothing there!"

I regretted going down as soon as I got there. The stench was indescribable. The stuffy heat of the hold made it even more unbearable than the smell on deck. Sweat was pouring off my body. I started to retch.

Luckily, I'd had nothing to eat that morning, so my stomach was empty. Gradually, my eyes grew accustomed to the darkness. I should have listened to Toshi. I think I screamed.

From then on, my memory is uncertain. What I saw and what Toshi saw were completely different. I don't know why it was just me who saw those things.

As soon as we got back to the shore, Toshi went straight to my father—the policeman.

"Somebody had been hiding in there," he told Dad. "Maybe they were doing some illegal fishing."

I couldn't understand what he was saying.

"They had a tank full of yellowtail. All dead now."

What's he talking about? I thought. *It wasn't just the yellowtail that were dead. It was people.*

I stood behind him, shaking my head in disbelief.

Even Dad couldn't keep on doing nothing now. Yoshi-nī, who was generally seen as the owner of the bay, wasn't back from his trip yet, but Dad picked up the telephone and called the police station in the nearest town.

I was relieved that the reality turned out to be what Toshi saw and not what I saw. But if what I saw wasn't real, then what was that appalling smell?

At first, I didn't know what it was I was looking at.

There were dozens of people lying on top of each other. The dim hold was packed with human bodies. Most were men. They wore shorts, but their chests were bare. The women wore shorts and T-shirts. I thought I could make out some small children among them too. The bodies were stiffer than the planks of the floor. Their skin was dark red, as if all their blood had hardened in an instant. Flies buzzed around them. White bubbles were wriggling around the people's mouths, as though their final exhalations, their last sighs, were continuing even now. But it wasn't just around their mouths. It was in their ears, their eyes, around their backsides too. Not bubbles at all, maggots. I immediately shut my eyes, but what I had seen burrowed its way past my eyelids, and deep inside my head. Together with the stench of decomposition, it took up its place in me and gave no sign of leaving. To drive the pile of bodies and their terrible stench from my mind, I screamed. I screamed with all the energy I had, so that every single thing would be driven out of me.

It was just then, I'm sure, that something began to flow from inside me. But it was a little later, when we'd left the Midori Maru and were going full throttle across the bay, that I remembered, and my relief came. My sweat dried quickly in the sea breeze, but the discomfort in my crotch remained.

From then on, Dad was very busy.

A lot of police came to investigate, not only from the town but from prefectural headquarters too. A Coast Guard cutter came to the bay and pulled the Midori Maru in to the quay.

Hatsue's Midori Maru had finally returned home. But her feelings must have been complicated. She frowned when she got back from the women's association trip and was told that the boat had been used by unauthorized migrants.

The villagers thronged to the quay to see what was going on. Mitsugu Azamui made his way through the crowd, right up to the police tape that surrounded the Midori Maru.

"See!" he said triumphantly. "I said there was a corpse!"

A few of the investigators shot him suspicious glances. The villagers just shook their heads. "There he goes again!" they laughed. But I couldn't laugh. It startled me when I heard him talking about his corpse again. Piles of dead bodies filled every corner of my mind. My spine ran cold. Clammy sweat dripped from my armpits and down my back. Before long, Mr. Kawano came rushing over and, with a sad face, pulled Mitsugu Azamui out of the crowd.

Dad was in the garden being spoken to by a group of senior officers.

"Yes, sir...yes, sir...yes, sir," he said, nodding forlornly.

The Silica Four were out on the road, glancing worriedly in Dad's direction. At the same time, they were enjoying a chat with Dad's predecessor, Mr. Yamamoto, whom they hadn't seen in a long time. Shiro was looking bored, wandering back and forth over the bridge.

Several national TV networks had sent crews to the village and they were interviewing Yoshi-nī. He had just gotten back from his trip. I saw him, surrounded by microphones and cameras, talking about something or other. His obese face was bright red. As he spoke, he kept trying to blow back strands of hair that had fallen across his fat forehead. Hachi-nī was

standing enviously outside the ring of cameras. Tiger Jeet Singh was always destined to be Abdullah the Butcher's sidekick.

According to the news on TV I saw later, a man who'd come to Japan on the Midori Maru was arrested in Kita Kyushu City as part of a group of unauthorized Chinese migrants. From him, the police found out that there'd been twenty-nine people packed into the boat's small hold. It was an unusually large number for a single trip. One of the TV stations broadcast a short documentary on Chinese people-smuggling organizations, but from what I saw of it, there was nothing specifically about the Midori Maru.

Once the fuss began to die down, Dad was pretty depressed for a while.

He'd been criticized for not doing anything about the unidentified boat for nearly a month. His salary would be docked. And he still hadn't paid off the damage to his new car.

"It's a disaster!" he said, his head in his hands.

"No point moaning about it now," said Mom bluntly.

"The repairs are going to cost a fortune," he said.

"Nobody to blame but yourself," she retorted.

"Dad," I said. "What were you going to say to Mr. Yoshida? You kept saying you wanted to talk to him."

"Oh that? Well, I… I was going to ask him to tell the children not to shoot rockets at Toshiko-bā's house. Mr. Kawano's been asking me to do something about it. Some of the women have too. But I didn't think the kids would stop if I told them. Mr. Yoshida's

local, so I thought they might listen to him. But I can't think about all that now!"

Toshiko-bā—the sound of her name made me a bit sad. I'd just been talking to Toshi about her. He'd never shot rockets at her house; he'd never even thought of doing so. Maybe if Toshi and I worked together we'd be able to have some effect. I wanted to hear more about her from Mr. Kawano. And the next time I saw Toshiko-bā I'd say hello.

"Well, Miki, it's no good," said Dad with a groan. "You won't be able to go to a private high school. I'm just telling you now."

"What about me?" asked Keiji.

"Same goes for you. It's hopeless. Everything's hopeless."

"Nonsense!" said Mom with a smile. "I'll get a job. We'll be fine. Just leave it to me."